One
Cog
Out
of
Synch

One Cog Out of Synch

99 One-a-Day Stories for Barbara Ann

John Hastings

Beaver's Pond Press, Inc.
Edina, Minnesota

ISBN 1-59298-088-0

Library of Congress Catalog Number: 2004097558

Printed in the United States of America

First Printing: October 2004

08 07 06 05 04   5 4 3 2 1

Beaver's Pond Press, Inc.

7104 Ohms Lane, Suite 216
Edina, MN 55439
(952) 829-8818
www.beaverspondpress.com

to order, visit www.BookHouseFulfillment.com or call
1-800-901-3480. Reseller discounts available.

Contents

Preface

I knew from the moment I first saw Barbara Ann that we'd be together. When I passed through the doorway into the crowded room something within drew my immediate attention to the slender smiling brunette sitting among so many strangers. I'd never had this kind of eerie feeling before but it was immediately clear that she'd be an important part of my life. And the feeling was correct. She was the warmest and most kindhearted person I'd ever met. We fell madly in love and stayed madly in love for over thirty years. Even with my busy career and raising our children there was always an inner excitement when we were together. I was as much enamored with Barbara Ann the day she died as the day we met.

When the youngest of our children left the nest we looked forward to a long future together. We bought a little honeymoon-type house up north where we would spend much of our time when I retired. It was a dream come true.

Then in so short a time Barbara was diagnosed with cancer. I retired immediately to be with her through a battle that slowly diminished our view from optimism to only slight hope. Upon Barbara's wishes we moved full-time to the little place on the lake where she died in my arms at age fifty-three.

I languished in isolation, depression, and grief for two years, as if just waiting to die myself. It seemed that my life had been like a wonderful book but that the final chapter had ended and I was awkwardly trying to keep it going. Then one day came an epiphany of sorts—probably of Barbara's doing—and I knew I would restart my life and dedicate it to making the world a bit happier.

One night after I was well into my new lifestyle I was reflecting on Barbara's and my last months together and recalled a project that made her happy. I had written a short story nearly every day to help raise her spirits. I knew exactly what she liked, something fun and tricky. Each day at the conclusion of the reading she'd say, "I love you, John." This brought tears to my eyes but also created the inner strength to make a happy story the next day in the midst of a situation of unimaginable fear and sorrow. I tried to keep the stories varied and whimsical as if removing us for a few minutes to another world.

When pondering on how much Barbara loved to make people happy, I realized that maybe these stories could be a part of her legacy and also fit my goal of creating happiness for others.

My hope is that in putting these stories in the form of a book, Barbara can know how our love for each other is making other people just a bit happier.

One
Cog
Out
of
Synch

Loser

On our honeymoon, Barbara and I watched a romantic movie filmed on the road from Rangoon to Mandalay.

"Second Placer" would have been a more appropriate moniker because that's where he always seemed to be: second in school academics, second-string in athletics, and second in about every contest he ever entered. But "Loser" just sounded better so that's how his classmates tagged him and that's what stuck. He took it good naturedly, the vein in which it was intended. "Second isn't that bad," he rationalized; he could live with it.

And second place turned out not to be so bad. He graduated second in his class, married his second choice of girls, and got a second-rate job at a second-rate company where he eventually rose to second in command. In the interim he often scored second place at local golf tournaments, sat second at his bridge club, and was second in line for several community awards. In general he was second-best at everything he did.

On the second day of the second month on his forty-second birthday, he got a most fortuitous phone call. He had been chosen as a contestant for a major quiz show. In the following weeks he placed second in the preliminaries and made it to the grand playoff that would be televised nationally. When the big night came he breezed through each question until only he and another contestant were left. Tension mounted as he was asked his final question: get it right and he was the grand winner; get it wrong and it was yet another second place.

"What," slowly asked the host "is the former name of Yangon." A shiver rushed through his body. He knew the answer. It was "Rangoon." He had just read a book about the road between Rangoon and Mandalay.

"Yes, yes," he thought to himself, "Rangoon to Mandalay and Rangoon became Yangon. Yes, yes!" The thought of him losing the moniker "Loser" raced through his mind and excited him. Then he tried to say "Rangoon" but to his horror nothing came out. He couldn't get the word to leave his mouth. He tried again and again. The time clock neared zero. In desperation he took one last powerful breath and, booming forth for the whole world to hear, his answer erupted . . . "MANDALAY."

Farm Philosopy

Personified animals made Barbara laugh.

A cow and a chicken stood by the side of the barn deeply engrossed in one of their regular philosophical discussions. Today the topic was reincarnation. The chicken began by saying that when he died he'd like to be reborn once again as a chicken. "I'm treated well," he said, "and have a nice home and I never have to work. It's really quite an ideal life and I feel good that I'm contributing my part to society by helping feed humans with my eggs. Even my eventual death will not be futile. I'll make a fine chicken dinner for some hungry family."

"I feel the same way," replied the cow. "I'd like to be another cow. Well, maybe a more interesting color than this boring brown. But we cows get to stand around all day and eat grass and talk and enjoy the outdoors and, at night, we have a fine shelter and plenty of company. Our milk is surely a good contribution, and when we die we each provide the meat for maybe a thousand hamburgers and the leather to make belts and shoes and jackets. Not only that, but we make our farmers happy by bringing them money for our sale and a profit to the butchers to boot."

"But maybe the best thing," added the chicken, "is that, unlike humans, who have to live into a painful and crippled old age, we live only our best years and in health and happiness."

"Yes," said the cow, "it would be a horror to come back as a human. They have to work most of their lives and then they can't even do the pleasing things like provide milk or eggs."

"And when they do die it makes everyone sad and cry," added the chicken. "And not only that but it costs money!"

"But there are some good things about being a human, I suppose," replied the cow, "such as⸺"

Just then a minivan drove by on the gravel road that passes the farm. Inside was a family from the city enjoying the rural countryside. "Hey, Dad," said a young boy in the back seat. "Look at that cow and chicken by the side of that barn. What do you think they're doing?"

"Oh," replied the dad, "probably discussing the weather." The van filled with laughter.

On the Slopes

Barbara especially enjoyed a tricky ending.

Slowly sliding, gliding down the ivory slope, leaving swirling traces in the creamy white. Swerving past the highest peak—no place to venture now or any day. Faster now, now slower to manipulate the pimplish mounds, bouncing gently over the larger ones and cringing through the field of smaller imperfections. Careful now as the down slope looms ahead, avoiding the thick bristly growth above the lip.

Head raises in expectation and suddenly Swoosh, over the edge and down, down, down, soaring and blowing through waves of undisturbed foamy white. At this speed beware of the long neck of mounds to the left! Faster, faster! Then deceleration and gently sliding to a stop well into the plateau.

But no time to pause on this bright morning. Hurriedly, the lofty airborne trip back to the top for another descent, and another, and another until tracks cover the face of the once pristine range. No hesitation , no reluctance in whisking to the other side of the high peak where not a single blade mark has scarred the silken flow. Once again on fresh terrain the glides, the swirls, the swerves . . . and the soaring.

Finally, a bit dulled by the ordeal, leaving the exhausted slopes until tomorrow, today's shave is over for this razor.

Aardvark

More animals and more removal from reality.

The aardvark, better known as the anteater, nearly didn't make it onto Noah's ark. The ark was going to be pretty darn full and Noah seriously questioned the wisdom of inviting ants and anteaters since they were both on the endangered species list and probably wouldn't last much longer anyway. It was common knowledge that the anteater had become so adept at eating ants that the ant population was dwindling rapidly. It was only a matter of time until the last one would be gobbled up. Then, of course, the anteater would have no food and he too would become extinct.

But Noah's wife chaired the local Animal's Rights League and through feminine manipulations, which curiously were left out of the Bible's version of the story, she convinced Noah to allow a pair of ants and a pair of anteaters on board. But there was trouble right away. The ark's accommodations coordinator had arranged the stalls in alphabetical order and this put the ant and the anteater in adjacent quarters. The temptation for a tasty snack would certainly overcome the anteater and result in carnivorism, a major ark taboo. So the two ants were relocated to the deck below. Soon many other animals wanted to switch places. The antelopes and deer wanted to move to the kitchen so they could play on the range and the kangaroos thought they'd be more comfortable on the lowest deck, down under. But few changes were allowed and the trip started with many irritated voyagers.

One thing the coordinator had overlooked is that in moving the ants she had placed them in a stall directly below the anteater, and through a knothole in a floorboard they were a scrumptious sight. Mrs. Anteater tried to keep her hungry spouse from taking action that might get them kicked off ship, but her husband just could not resist. He rationalized that the ants were a drudge to society anyway, messing up picnics and running all over kitchen counters, and that their demise would be nothing but a benefit to the world. So one night when everyone was asleep he squeezed his long snout through the hole in the floor and sucked with all his might, attempting to get both ants in one inhalation.

What he couldn't have anticipated is that the day before the ants had noticed an eye peering through a hole in their ceiling, and as a precaution, had changed stalls with their neighbors, Mr. and Mrs. Rattlesnake. Mr. Rattlesnake was pulled from a sound sleep and sucked into the anteater's snout headfirst, with only his rattle still exposed.

The anteater jumped back in astonishment, the noisy rattle at the end of his snout violently shaking. Everyone on ship awoke and the clacking sound kept them awake all night. The animals were really ticked off at the anteater but not as much as the rattle-snake who was wedged deep in his snout.

The next day, the snake slid into the anteater's stomach but this merely changed the rattle from an irksome rapping to a hollow, cavernous echo. This irritable noise kept up throughout the trip and by journey's end every animal aboard hated the ant-eater. This is why today you don't see anteaters around playing with other animals. They are loners that are rarely sighted except when sneaking about isolated anthills.

And, oh yes, neither the ant nor the anteater became extinct. You see, evolution and mutations and all that genetic stuff are strange things. That rattlesnake's rattle permanently lodged onto the anteater's stomach and in future generations the species developed it as a lasting part of their anatomy. This became a godsend for the ant who now was vocally warned when its predator approached. The ants numbers increased almost to a bothersome level. Incidentally, most of them have an excellent auditory sense because the anteater quickly disposed of those who couldn't hear its rattle.

The end of this story, and its main point, is that at night when you hear a clicking sound coming from the woods and you think it's some kind of cricket or bug, often it's not. Often, it is the lonely aardvark.

Class Chaos

Barbara loved reading about politics.

The scrolls do not cite a date but the best guess is that the following events took place in the days of ancient Persia. They tell of a band of about fifty warriors who, on returning from a battle, became lost and inadvertently wandered deep into uncharted land to the east. After a lonely trek of nearly a year they came upon an unknown kingdom that consisted of a large city surrounded by farmland. Their original plan was to ask for food and shelter. But upon discovering that the kingdom had no military, they decided to conquer. It took only a few hours and the kingdom was in their control.

The warriors soon found that this was a very pleasant place to reign. The rich upper class had the very finest of quarters, living conditions, and extravagances, and the lower class seemed overworked but content to serve. There was no crime. Everyone seemed quite happy and had been for many generations. Few changes would have to be made.

Well, that is until the new leader discovered what he considered a serious flaw. It seems that there were only two classes, upper and lower, but that on the first day of every year they changed places. That's right, all of the nobles went to the fields or to the city worker jobs and all the farmers and workers advanced to the life of luxury with official positions and an opulent lifestyle. This was the strangest thing the new leader had ever heard and he listened carefully to its explanation. "You see," said the former leader, "the year that we are in the lower class we develop good hardworking ethics and we enjoy serenity and health and good old-fashioned fellowship and values. We build character of both mind and body. Then in the year we are in the upper class we relax and enjoy the fruits of our labor. We finish our official duties capably by noon each day and then we overindulge in our wildest whimsies and don't feel the least guilt in eating, drinking, and being ever so merry."

The new leader didn't like this system at all. It would mean that he and his band would only rule in alternating years, and besides, he was spooked by its oddity. "No," he declared, "we will all stay as we are today; no more of this bizarre switching routine." And so it was to be for five years. But that proved to be a bad decision. Having nothing to look forward to, the lower class became sad and resentful and both their work and values suffered. And the upper class did no better. Most became overweight and lazy drunkards whose capacity to rule dwindled.

Foreseeing disaster, the leader knew a change was necessary. He couldn't go back to the old switching method. The upper class was now in no shape for physical work and the lower class was so bitter that it would probably want five years on top instead of one. No, he needed a fresh plan and eventually decided upon an entirely new system. Except for a small group of capable upper-class people and a small group of lower-class people for the most menial or rigorous work, the kingdom would be made up of one large middle class.

It seemed like a good idea and, as a compromise, it did function acceptably. After several years there was still peace in the kingdom and most people were moderately happy. Most people worked moderately hard and celebrated moderately and even had a mix of moderately earnest values. And once in a while, if you did some searching, you could find a very hardworking person, or someone having a roaring good time, or an especially capable leader, or even a person of good solid values.

Epiphany

This actually happened to me, not Joe.

Joe left the church that evening deep in thought. The group discussion had been on the nature of charity. The topic drifted onto altruism, or whether there exists any charitable act that does not contain some selfishness. This question bothered Joe because he had always been a giving person. Even when he donated money he did so anonymously. But he now wondered if in his charity he was trying to make himself feel good or maybe buying the grace of a higher power. He'd never thought of this before and didn't think it was true but he couldn't be certain. For four blocks he walked and pondered and then paused, closing his eyes for a few seconds and said a brief prayer.

The grocery store was just ahead. Joe decided to buy a sandwich to take home. He checked his cash and found two crisp new five-dollar bills. "What the heck," he thought. "I'll make it a night and ten dollars is just right; five for a good sandwich and five for lottery scratch-off tickets." He rarely bought these tickets and never won more than a dollar, but for some reason the time felt right. So he stopped in the gas station and bought five one-dollar cards. He paused under the lights outside the station and began to scratch away. One, two, three, four, and no luck. Just as he was about to play his last ticket a stranger approached him. He was holding cash in one hand and told Joe that he had bought twenty-one dollars worth of gas, had only sixteen dollars in cash and his credit card had been refused. In a very humbling manner he asked Joe for five dollars.

Instantly Joe began to think, "Gee, I've been stopped before in this part of town and asked for change or even a dollar. But five bucks?! What kind of a scam is this?" But then in an instant he recalled his recent mental dilemma on charity and said to himself, "What in the world am I thinking ? This guy needs five bucks and I've got five bucks." He gave the stranger his last five. Only seconds later he scratched off his last lottery card. It was a sixty-dollar winner.

Glass Canoe

My career was in developing new products. Barbara was happy when I was creating something new. And so was I.

Although George and George Jr. were father and son, they had one glaring difference. George had an optimistic view of most undertakings while his son was cautious to the point of pessimism. You could say that the elder always "saw the glass half full" and the younger, the glass "half empty." An example might be when George, whose house was on a little lake, had the idea for a transparent canoe. Those were the days before modern plastics and the only crystal-clear material available was glass. But this didn't bother him. He thought only of the novelty of being able to see the lake bottom and fish below him while paddling. Bubbling with enthusiasm he called his son, who was a grown man himself, to discuss the notion.

It was predictable that George Jr. would try to dampen his father's enthusiasm. "First of all, Dad," he began, "it's going to be almost impossible to find a glassmaker who can form a canoe for you. And second, even if you do it's going to cost a fortune. But worst of all, a glass canoe would crack and shatter if you hit a rock or any other object in the lake. It would probably break just hitting the dock. No, Dad, this is definitely not one of your better ideas!"

But George was not easily discouraged. He did find a glassmaker and did have his transparent canoe made. His son was correct about the cost but it turned out be worth the price. For twenty years George enjoyed an underwater view of his lake that brought him great delight. He was very careful about hitting obstacles and the craft stayed intact the entire time. It was only when he was in his seventies and arthritis made it impossible to paddle that the canoe sat idle.

But George's mind wasn't idle. He had another brainstorm, a domed skylight for his living room. You guessed it, the dome would be his canoe inverted. This glass boat had shown him the depths of the earth before and now it would show him the heights of the heavens. Again his son felt it was a terrible idea. "It will look odd, cost a fortune to install, and worst of all, it would shatter to pieces during a hailstorm."

But again his father was not discouraged and had his skylight installed. And it turned out to look fitting and was certainly a conversation piece. It stayed intact until the day he died, fifteen years later. This may have been because it hadn't hailed, not once in all those years. The first hail came when his son inherited and moved into the house. And then it was a doozy. George Jr. was right. The glass skylight didn't have a chance.

Little Legs

Barbara loved stories about animals,
especially small animals.

One mother duck and her seven little ducklings—how quaintly they waddled from their nest in the woods, across the road, and to the water's edge. But they walked a bit slower than one might expect because the smallest duckling, a little female whose legs were noticeably shorter than the others, governed their pace. She became known as "Little Legs." As hard as she tried, Little Legs could not keep up with her mother and siblings, so they all had to slow down to keep her within the group. This perturbed many of her brothers and sisters because they were always eager to get to the lake for a day of fun.

Storms were rare in this part of the country, but on one particular day huge clouds loomed in the west. The duck family woke early because they knew that they would have only a couple of hours on the lake before they must retreat to the safety of the woods. For the first time the ducklings actually voiced their disgust at being slowed down by Little Legs. "We only have a couple of hours to swim, Mom," they argued. "Let's leave her in the nest just for today." But the mother duck was compassionate and refused to leave her littlest offspring behind because of a handicap over which she had no control.

So the group waddled slowly out of the woods. Just as they were about to cross the road a huge truck roared past them. They were all quite dazed by the sudden close call and stood for a moment in shock. Then their mother turned to the group and said something that they would never forget: "Had we left Little Legs behind we would have been right in the middle of the road and all been killed. Her slow pace saved our lives!" From that moment Little Legs was revered by her family and they never complained about her slowness again.

Several years later Little Legs was a mother herself and had a group of seven ducklings of her own and lived in a nest in the woods near the lake. Her legs had now grown to normal size but she, like her mother, had a duckling whose legs were very short, who was called Little Legs, and whose siblings complained about her. And again one day, clouds loomed in the west and the little ones beseeched the mother to leave "Little Legs" in the nest for just one day. The mother quieted them and told her story of the truck. Silent and impressed, they were now ready to wait for Little Legs. Then, at the end of the story, the mother surprisingly added, "But the odds of this happening again are a million-to-one so we will leave her behind today."

Henhouse

Yes, sweetheart, these do sound like some of our neighbors.

The chickens will sleep tonight. They have built two ingenious traps and placed one each at the front and back doors. Even the foxiest fox will not be eating chicken tonight. Then, at just after midnight, comes a clatter and commotion at the front door. For the first time in the history of this farm a fox has been caught, both front legs secured by a strong woven rope. The delighted chickens jump from their roosts and gather round. "We's goin' to change our eatin' habits, girls," cheers the oldest hen. "It'll be fox burgers tonight and fox stew tomorrow." They flapped their wings in unison and jumped up and down with joy.

"Wait, wait, wait," the fox interrupts their gayety, "you ladies have this all wrong. I'm not a fox!"

"You looks like a fox and you talks like a fox," laughs the old hen. "That means you is a fox, a fox that was lookin' to have a fat chicken dinner."

"No, no, no," insists the fox in a shy and innocent voice. "Sure, I look like a fox and talk like a fox. That's because I'm related to the fox. You see, I'm a phox, spelled with a 'ph.' But us phoxes aren't anything like our kin. We're vegetarians and never eat meat. I'm new to this area and was just stoppin' by to introduce myself."

"We's goin' to eat you anyway," one of the chickens in the back yells and they all nod in agreement.

"You wouldn't want to do that, ma'am," pleads the fox. "Phox meat is very bitter 'cause of our diets of garlic and chokecherries and it will surely make you sick. Please believe me, you'd best let me go. I'll return to my poor wife and kids and never come back." The fox's story becomes more and more convincing and the chickens finally decide to let him free. But as soon as the ropes are loosened, he leaps up and grabs a plump hen by the neck. From the corner of his mouth snickers an evil voice, "It's chicken dinner for this bachelor tonight."

"Stop!" yells the oldest hen. "You won't have a chicken dinner this night!

"And just why not?" responds the fox sarcastically.

"Well," answers the hen after a bit of hesitation, "because we ain't chickens. We's what you call phrickens, spelled with a 'ph,' a relative of the chicken. They call us phrickens 'cause we isn't no phricken good to eat."

The fox laughs. "You old gals don't really think you can outfox the fox, do you?" He heads toward the back door. And then in an instant, wham! he's caught in the second trap. The chicken in his grasp leaps to freedom. The startled fox looks up at the group of hens and in a shy and innocent voice beseeches, "Ladies, ladies, ladies."

But the oldest hen quickly mutes his words by shoving a large egg in his mouth. In a stern voice she cackles loudly, "We's goin' to have a phox pheast tonight, girls!" and glancing at the fox adds, "And that's with a 'ph.'"

Influence

Some years earlier I had written Barbara a little book of mystery stories. She loved a mystery.

She was frightened and worried, not knowing what to do about her only son, Paul. He was a very bright boy but had lost all interest in education when he came under the influence of two new friends, both street hoods and petty thieves. Paul was at the age where this type seemed "cool" and macho to him. The two friends often hung around the smoke shop where he worked part time, an ideal location for the two to peddle small amounts of drugs.

Paul's mother knew that it was only a matter of time before they'd be caught and Paul was certain to be implicated. But she just couldn't get him to listen to common sense. She was overwhelmed with a sense of guilt that he had no father image at home, but his father had abandoned her when Paul was born. If she could only locate him, maybe he'd be of some help.

One evening a few nights later she ran home from a fortune-teller who had just opened a little shop down the street, and frantically grabbed her boy and his sister Ruth and begged them to stay at home the following day. "I have just been given a terrible omen," she sobbed. "It says that one of my children will be hurt tomorrow if they're not together. It says they will die! You have to stay here in the house together all day."

They agreed. But late the next afternoon Paul got a call from his boss at the tobacco shop who was feeling ill and begged him to mind the store just until seven o'clock when another boy would come on duty. Feeling strongly that all fortune-tellers were frauds, Paul wasn't worried about the omen and, against the pleas of his sister, he left.

Just before seven a man with a slight but noticeable limp entered the shop and bought several cartons of cigarettes. He paid from a large wad of bills and then said he had another errand and asked if he could pick up his purchase half an hour later. Paul's two friends, who had been hanging around all afternoon, observed the transaction. After the man left, they took no time in planning a simple scheme. The three of them would follow the man after he returned and make an easy hit. Paul, who would be relieved in ten minutes, reluctantly agreed. Just then the phone rang. It was Paul's mother, frantically crying and screaming. "You must hurry home, son," she pleaded. "I came home and found Ruth on the floor. I don't know if she's breathing. I called the ambulance but I need you now!"

He raced home in terror. Was his sister going to die? Was the omen true and was it his fault for leaving her alone? Luckily, his sister had just fainted.

The emergency was over, but not the impact of the omen. The next morning Paul learned that his two friends had been shot to death in self-defense by a stranger with a limp who disappeared from the scene. "My god," thought Paul, "I was the one who was going to die! I would have been shot if I hadn't left." He was shaken deeply and decided to quit his job and concentrate on school. A week later, his mother again returned from the fortune-teller but this time beaming.

"You are going to be educated and become honorable and wealthy, my son," she cried in delight. And this came to be true. Twenty years later Paul was a gifted and successful surgeon and the pride of his aged mother.

Late one afternoon, a tattered old gray-haired man made his way into Paul's office and claimed to be his father. Even though he had never seen his father, something seemed familiar in the face and this made Paul hesitate. Perhaps it was some type of family resemblance. The man showed documented proof and Paul was aghast. He scolded the man long and mercilessly and then shoved him from his office. "You abandoned me and my mother and sister nearly forty years ago, you wretched old bastard!" he shouted before slamming the door, "Don't come around here looking for anything because I owe you nothing! Nothing. You hear that? Nothing!"

A slight smile appeared on the face of the old man. "Nothing?" he mumbled, walking slowly down the corridor with a slight but noticeable limp.

Jaded

*Barbara was a strong believer in her higher power but
enjoyed very much talking about different theologies.*

Theirs was a very happy marriage with only one tiny flaw. He
was a matter-of-fact man, a scientist and atheist. She, on the
other hand, was a romantic, knew nothing of science and was
very pious. But they were in love and managed to work around
their differences quite amicably. Wishing for harmony he usually conceded on issues where their beliefs collided, even to the
point where he agreed to raise their young daughter with religion. He went to church with them regularly, but pondered on
lofty physics problems during the sermons.

One morning at breakfast their little girl asked her mother
if they would go up to heaven when they died. "Of course," was
the reply. But the little girl mused "People on the other side of
the Earth can't go up to heaven because their up is really our
down." This type of reasoning obviously came from the genetics
of the father and it quite suddenly had an impact upon him. An
epiphany you might say.

"My word!" he proclaimed, "I just had a breakthrough
thought! According to Einstein, the universe is curved. If this is
so, then an object moving skyward directly away from us must
eventually meet at a common place with an object moving skyward on the other side of the globe, say China. In fact, any object
moving skyward from any point on the earth must converge at a
common place. My word! This might sound naive but I think I

can figure out the mathematics and physics to prove this theory." He was elated and ran enthusiastically to his office. Meanwhile the mother was also thinking and in a few minutes she had her own epiphany.

"If he's right," she romanticized, " then that place where everything leaving the Earth goes has to be heaven. If he can prove that there is one place where everything meets, then we will have scientific proof for heaven. This could be a whole new religion. I have to get to church and talk to Reverend Beck."

The proof of the man's theory proved to be more lengthy and difficult than expected but at the constant urging of his wife it was finally complete ten years later, and he gained worldwide acclaim in the scientific community. It became known as the Hanson Theory of Unrelativity and could be simply expressed in the equation E=GAD. In the meantime his wife had earned a master's degree in theology and was deeply involved in and ready to launch her new religion called Where Heaven Only Abides or WHOA for short.

He became famous and she became famous and the daughter was very pleased that they'd given her full credit for starting the whole thing. But they just couldn't leave well enough alone. With her support, he continued to work on his theory. What they both really wanted to find was just where in the cosmos existed this magical converging point. His interest was in furthering his knowledge and hers in finding the location of heaven to better direct her prayers. When he finally solved the problem he rushed to inform his wife. "Honey," he said solemnly, "any object leaving the Earth skyward will eventually return to its origin."

"Good heavens on Earth!" she screamed.

Today their marriage has never been so good. Their differences in beliefs have evaporated. They are both strong and loyal followers of the same theology: reincarnation.

Mind Play

*Barbara had a cleaver mind and especially
enjoyed stories involving mental trickery.*

Barton's life might best be characterized as one long cerebral play in three acts. He displayed early signs of becoming an accomplished artist. His paintings were beautiful and filled with feeling. But he also had another promising talent. He was the wizard of his high school and college debate teams and was rarely challenged successfully on an argument or viewpoint. He became very well read and could converse on most any subject with detail and eloquence.

When making a career decision, Barton took his friend's advice that the power of his knowledge and logic would provide more rewards in this modern world than his ability to draw. This decision drew Barton into politics, where by virtue of his oratory he won his way to the position of mayor. But when he eventually ran for governor he was badly beaten by an opponent who was much his opposite: quiet, unassuming, and compromising. This shocked Barton. He had honed his wit and rhetoric for the big debate the day before the election and had never been in such a lopsided verbal contest, countering every point made by his adversary with a combination of logic and biting sarcasm. What had happened? How could he have lost?

Barton again consulted his friend and was shocked when told that he had been so dogmatic and unyielding in his viewpoints that he came across as a dictatorial and ruthless zealot. "Your opinions have become so rigid and adamant," conveyed his friend, "that you appear domineering, bullheaded, and unlikable. You must expand your logic to become more even-keeled." You couldn't tell by his demeanor, but Barton really was a quite sensitive and compassionate person and these words bothered him greatly. He vowed never again to argue or debate without consideration.

Barton was, however, a bright and educated man and found himself often having strong opinions on many issues. To solve this bothersome trait he made a decision to purposely argue with himself with equal vigor on both sides of any question, regardless of his original instincts. To his fascination he always found merit on each side. In the past he had never even considered the opposite point of view but now he found he could debate and, indeed, become just as ethically convinced of its legitimacy. He began practicing this new exercise on issues ranging from minor daily concerns to lofty political and philosophical problems. Over the years the process became second nature.

The only problem with this new approach was that Barton eventually found himself hopelessly lost in the indecisive center of all issues, small and large. He believed strongly in everything and strongly in nothing. He wanted to write a book but couldn't because he had no conclusive viewpoints, only strong and conflicting ideas on all sides. He wanted to marry but couldn't; mentally, he indulged every virtue of marriage but also the merits on remaining single, and as usual fell somewhere in the middle with no conclusive action. And probably worse was that in politics he became known as wishy-washy and feeble and lost election after election.

In desperation he once again consulted his friend who suggested that logic had actually been the culprit all along. "Abandon logic and rely on your art," he recommended. Having no better option Barton followed this advice wholeheartedly.

Ten years later the two crossed paths again. His friend was delighted to find Barton looking great, in mental bliss, and able to make even difficult decisions with ease. Barton assured his friend that his success was due entirely to the advice he was given earlier. "Great!" said his friend proudly. "When can I see some of your paintings?" Barton replied that he hadn't painted in decades. "What?" exclaimed his friend, "I advised that you abandon logic and rely on your art!"

"Art?" replied Barton. "I thought you said heart."

Klem's Revenge

Barbara and I had talked about the futility of holding a grudge and how difficult it is to resist.

There were two large department stores downtown and it was destined that within a year there would be only one. With the advent of shopping centers and mini-malls, core city traffic could no longer support both of the large and historic stores. Klem had worked for one of them, Cooper's, for thirty years and had been recently laid off because of slow business. He was furious that the cuts were arbitrary and took into account neither his loyalty nor his long years of service. He felt that old man Cooper had always disliked him and Klem, especially now, despised the ruthless and clever old tightwad. Oh, how he would love to see Dixon's Department Store be the survivor in the upcoming battle.

Klem applied for a position at Dixon's but wasn't hopeful of getting it and spent much of his time in fantasies of revenge on Cooper. Then one day, while visiting a friend in a neighboring state, a plan arose. His friend was a kind and gentle man who loved to make people happy. He had created little tokens made from poker chips on which were affixed round labels with the printed words "NICE DAY." He would hand one to a clerk or passerby or a person on a park bench and simply say, "Here, have a NICE DAY." And it worked. Not only did it add a bit of novel enjoyment to the receiver but made his friend very happy. Klem was watching this act in action when the idea hit.

He learned how to make the "Nice Day" tokens and upon returning home printed up five thousand of his own. The only difference was that Klem added a smaller label on the back of the chip that read, "Redeemable at Cooper's for $5 in merchandise." He was in sheer ecstasy when feverishly applying the labels. He knew that Cooper wouldn't honor them and that in turning them down he would create hundreds of frustrated and dissatisfied customers. This might just create the little difference that would make them lose the battle for survival. With delight he could picture the face of a bewildered and angry Cooper. "Aha," smiled Klem, "I have plenty of time and if I can hand out a hundred tokens a day they will last for nearly two months." But he had only the time for a week of handouts as he was offered and accepted a new job in management at Dixon's.

He, of course, wasn't present when the barrage of tokens hit the counters at Cooper's. The clerks didn't know what to tell customers and the old man was immediately consulted. "That damn Dixon!" the old white haired retailer mused, "He's behind this!" He scratched his head for a moment in thought and then proclaimed, "Honor the tokens. Honor them all." The staff was amazed at his decision, feeling that it would do nothing but put Cooper's further in the red and be the last straw in their downfall.

But it turned out to be just the opposite. The redemptions, which Cooper began to term as "his promotion," created a whole new wave of business and goodwill. Dixon's didn't have a chance. Their business dropped dramatically and a month later they closed.

And Klem? Well, he was once again without a job and few prospects. It didn't look good on his resume having lasted just a month in his first management position. His financial concerns were eased a bit, however, when he made regular redemptions at Cooper's with his four thousand remaining NICE DAY tokens.

Lucidity

Although we had hope until the end, Barbara
liked to talk about life and death. She enjoyed
stories that spanned a lifetime.

Peter was a quiet and somewhat mysterious young man of thirty-five who spent most of his time reading or taking long walks. When both of his parents died unexpectedly, he inherited the large estate and mansion on which he had idled for so many years. Whether it was from something that was triggered upon his parent's death or something inherent in Peter himself nobody knows, but Peter began a most unusual project that he labored on until his own death forty years later. One bright morning he removed the grass from a large portion of the spacious front lawn to expose a circular area of rich black loam. On the second morning he appeared with a shovel and began digging the dirt from this large circle. He repeated this operation for a month until he had created a hole fifty feet in diameter and nearly four feet deep. Passersby and neighbors became very curious. What was Peter making and with all his money why wasn't he having it done with machinery by hired workers? Only a few people knew Peter and then only casually. When making inquiries, they learned only that the project was confidential. Speculation abounded. Most thought it would be the beginning of a spectacular structure that he felt duty-bound to create himself, probably in honor of his parents. Others thought it was going to be a magnificent pond.

The routine continued every day for the next year, Peter digging from sunrise to sunset. He had an elaborate and expensive conveyer rig installed that carried the dirt from the depths of the hole to its top and along two rails to the side of the mansion where a truck was waiting to periodically haul it away. The hole was now over forty feet deep and speculations turned to some kind of structure that would surely have underground levels. Some felt that Peter was eccentric enough to be digging a bomb shelter. But after ten years the hole was four hundred feet deep and no one had a reasonable guess. The project became so bizarre that every day people would stop and peer down at the slender and now quite muscular Peter toiling tirelessly. That year a local radio station had a contest to guess the purpose of Peter's Pit as it was now often called. Responses ranged from a missile silo to a route to China to a hole for the world's largest flagpole.

After a total of forty years the digging stopped, leaving the excavation nearly fifteen hundred feet deep. Looking from its rim into the depths one could no longer see Peter's shape, only a dim light coming from the nadir of the abyss. Then late one afternoon as Peter, an old man by now, emerged from the pit and wearily walked back to the mansion for supper, he paused and dropped over from a stroke. He was rushed to the hospital, where he remained in the intensive care unit to pass his final hours.

A thousand miles away, in a similar intensive care unit, lay an old farmer who opened his eyes one last time before passing and smiled contentedly. He thought of all the people he had fed for so many years.

On the other side of the country, lay a musician in a similar condition who contented himself with thoughts of all the thousands he had entertained during his lifetime.

On the opposite coast, a doctor lay dying with happy memories of all the lives he'd saved.

In another hospital the last thoughts of an old waitress were of all those she had served.

But in Peter's hospital lay Peter who in one final moment of lucidity yelled in a tired voice, "What in the hell was I thinking!?"

Mutant

Maybe my mind was dwelling on lifetimes.

As if the recipient of some mutated gene, Frank was born with an ungodly distorted face. The rest of his body was normal but, even as a baby, most people cringed when looking upon his countenance. His eyes were of two different shades of brown and black and bulged half an inch from their sockets. His forehead was as rough as sandpaper and covered with large pocks, each sprouting an eerie stubby hair. His nose was huge and crooked and his mouth distorted and slanted. All of this was canvassed on an oversized and squared head that grew only patches of hair. His parents were too poor to have any remedial work done so he suffered terrible humiliation all though his younger years. Frank was just so gruesome that even the most benevolent and understanding of people had difficulty remaining calm when facing him. And, because of blood abnormalities, the future didn't look bright either since the prognosis for living anything other than a short life was poor.

However, Frank did become accepted when, in his twenties, he joined the circus and was a hit attraction under the billing Frank-in-Stein. His act consisted of him being placed in a huge glass beer stein, growling and distorting his face even more than normal. For fifteen years he enjoyed his life, but rarely ventured from the confines of the circus and his comrades. He spent long hours at his favorite pastime, handcrafting wood, and saved his money earnestly. When he had finally saved enough he spent it all on an expensive and extensive facelift surgery. And it worked marvelously. After several months of healing, Frank was normal-looking, if not borderline handsome. He was no longer of value to the circus but was quickly noted for his woodworking talent. He became a sculptor of some note. He fell in love and settled down to a wonderful life. Wonderful, that is, except that he couldn't help but be somewhat haunted by the prediction of an abbreviated life expectancy. But after reaching age fifty he no longer worried and lived to his late seventies.

Old and dying, Frank rested in his favorite stuffed chair one evening when Death appeared. "Are you ready, Frank?" asked Death.

"Yes, I am ready," responded Frank, "but could I ask you one question first?"

"Of course."

"I was supposed to die early in life from some blood abnormality. Why did you not call on me earlier?"

"Oh, I did Frank." replied Death. "I called on you once in your twenties and tried again in your thirties. But each time your face frightened me off."

Ornery Orville

*Only yesterday we were talking about how
most endeavors taken to an extreme go awry.*

O rville was one of those guys who's always complaining,
especially about the deficiencies of other people. You
couldn't talk to Orville without hearing at least one new tale of
how mankind was so stupid. He must have spent hours each day
observing and creating such ludicrous interpretations of human
nature. He might, for example, go off on a long oration about
people washing their hands after using the washroom. "You
shower in the morning and get clean," he would rage, "then you
put on not one, but two layers of clothes to keep any dirt or con-
taminant from reaching your private parts, and then after your
hands spend all day collecting grime and germs from everything
from money to doorknobs, you don't wash them before you con-
taminate your privates. No! You know what you do? You wash
them after! What could be more backwards?" Or he might rattle
on about more obscure things such as birthdays. "Birthday cards!"
he'd exclaim. "Why in the world do we give birthday cards? It's
not your birthday! You only have one birthday! That's the day
you're born! It's really an observance of a new year for you. We
should be giving Happy New Year cards!"

But his favorite cause was waste. He'd get downright mad
when talking about lawns and the energy and pollution wasted
on cutting them. "We have the technology to create grass that
only grows a few inches high but do we use it? Hell no! We'd put

the lawnmower companies out of business and the oil companies wouldn't sell as much gas! Can't do that, can we? Hell no!"

Friends knew never to mention packaging to Orville. He'd have your ear for an hour. "They put ten cents worth of soda in a fifteen-cent can or bottle and what do we do?" he'd scream. "We throw the fifteen-cent part away! And then we get on our high horses and brag about our concern for ecology and pollution and depletion of rain forests. And when we're finished patting ourselves on the back we eat at a fast-food joint and throw away a quarter's worth of paper bags and cups and napkins! Then we go home and read a dollar newspaper and throw that away! Are we nuts? Are we absolutely nuts?"

But one thing can be said for Orville. He did follow his own sentiments. He always washed his hands before instead of after using a washroom, always sent "Happy New Year" instead of birthday cards, had artificial turf instead of lawn, and always watched the news on TV instead of buying newspapers. He was also especially conscientious about wasting materials, and in particular, he avoided products with elaborate or expensive packaging.

But on the packaging issue Orville finally fell short. You'd think that in all his years of daily haranguing he had covered every possible issue on wasteful packaging. After his death, he was buried in a new five hundred-dollar suit and a three-thousand-dollar casket.

Recruits

Barbara liked stories with ironies or twists. and
sometimes I could tell what she'd prefer that day.

In the corner of the ornate reception hall, two gray-haired men introduced themselves. In an hour they'd both be awarded the coveted "Man of the Year" prize for distinguished lifetime services. Each of the five honorees would receive a raving introduction and a golden trophy and then be asked to summarize their achievements in a thirty-minute talk. These two found the time limit frustrating to describe such illustrious careers. One decided to make abbreviations and eliminate his introductory anecdote and the other opted talk faster than usual.

Unbeknownst to either man, they were the same age and their careers began in the same general area in Asia. Robert, the taller of the two, was eighteen when he was drafted into the army. This was a huge shock and disappointment. He was a brilliant and industrious young man and was looking forward to becoming a doctor. He wanted to devote his life to saving lives and was aghast at the thought of being part of a war where he may have to kill. Would he kill if imperiled? Probably not, he thought.

He detested being platoon leader, but his aptitude and natural ability were traits he could never camouflage; he naturally rose in rank. Robert just seemed to be the best at whatever he did. But now he was in a hopeless situation. He found himself in a muddy trench surrounded by enemy, and he, being platoon leader, was responsible for the safety of his men. He wasn't afraid to die but wanted badly to save his fellow soldiers.

A week later he arrived home to a hero's welcome. Newspapers and magazines bannered his gallant one-man attack that killed twenty enemy fighters and broke a hole in their defenses through which he and his men escaped. While still recovering from his injuries he was visited by a five-star general who beseeched him to enter officer's school and stay in the armed forces. The promise of rapid advancement and special attention were convincing and he decided to give it a try, at least for a while. Robert was good at everything he did and now, forty years later, he himself was a five-star general of considerable note.

The shorter man, Henry, was also in that war but he had volunteered. Although a brilliant boy with the aptitude to be successful in whatever vocation he endeavored, he had his heart set on being an army officer. He was a sportsman who loved hunting and his family had a long heritage of fighting for their country. He looked forward to hand-to-hand encounters with the enemy and volunteered for the most dangerous missions.

One night he was with a small assault group in a dense forest. It was considered a suicide mission and every soldier except Henry was frightened as they stormed toward the enemy position. Just as the assault began, Henry suddenly became entangled in underbrush where he fell. His head slammed against a tree stump and he was unconscious for almost a day. Luckily the attack had been successful and his cohorts had advanced several miles. It took a week for Henry to find their new position. When he did it was a horrible shock. Somehow he had been labeled a coward who had abandoned his platoon. A month later he was in front of a military court who found him guilty but let him go with a dishonorable discharge. When he got home Henry entered college and later medical school, mainly for its prestige. After forty years, he was a noted surgeon who had broken ground on several new procedures and successfully treated many people of renown.

Robert and Henry did not talk about their beginnings but were fascinated by each other's career. It was a very engrossing conversation filled with awe and envy that lasted right up to the ceremony. The ceremony was grand except that many members of the notable audience wondered why Robert's and Henry's speeches lacked the anticipated boastfulness and pride. And why did their speeches each last only five minutes?

Sky Society

Sometimes wordplay gets a "Boo."

A few of our time-tested phrases have come from sources that we would not expect. Take the example of clouds.

A young cloud floated lazily alongside his two white fluffy parents. It would have been a leisurely spring morning but today there was trouble. It seems the little cloud was insistent upon leaving his parents to see the world. They warned their little floater of the dangers in the sky, but to no avail. He was now of legal age and they could not force him to stay. Clouds don't carry much luggage, so all it took was a quick "goodbye" and he was off and away.

Most of the day was unexciting for the little cloud, the only action being a passing flock of geese. But then in late afternoon he saw hundreds of clouds speeding in the same direction. Many of them yelled "Come on along, we're going to make a storm." He didn't know what a storm was but it sounded exciting and he joined them. In about an hour they came to a giant dark cloud that was bellowing orders for the clouds to join them, which they anxiously complied with. At first the little white cloud was leery because of the confusion and the monstrous size of the accumulating mass. Eventually he drew close and was immediately thrust to the bottom of the swarm where it was dark and very cold. Then came violent clapping sounds as hundreds of clouds banged into each other. Sudden spears of light shot all the way to the Earth below.

The little cloud was frightened but unharmed until millions of drops of water fell from above and balls of ice tore through his soft body, making tatters and fragments of his delicate shape. Flash! Flash! Boom! Boom! More ice balls fell in a fury he had never dreamed possible. He shuttered in panic and cried for his parents.

Just as he felt his end was near, the turbulence stopped and the surviving clouds began to disperse. The sky became bright. The little cloud, weak and badly beaten, found himself alone. He drifted in the direction he thought was home, constantly calling for his mom and dad. It seemed like a miracle but just before dusk he did find them and was at last safe.

"My word!" exclaimed his mother. "What happened? You look just terrible."

"Yes," his father added as he nestled up to his ragged and hole-riddled son, "you look like you've been through hail."

Teresa

*Barbara was certain of her higher power. She also
liked the logic of asking happy older people for advice.*

Teresa had always marveled at her grandfather's optimism. He
put a positive slant on any problem or dilemma no matter
how severe. For example, when he lost his eyesight at age sixty,
he told Teresa "Everything's going to be just fine, sweetheart. I've
seen most everything in the world and I have a good memory."
Then when his memory started to go bad at age eighty, he told
her, "Everything's going to be fine, sweetheart. I'm very fortunate
to be able to learn things more than once now. Maybe I'll be able
to watch a video tonight and then enjoy it like new again next
week." And when he was bedridden a few years later he said that
he had been trying for over eighty years to find an excuse to stay
in bed all day.

This constant optimism annoyed many but it was always
refreshing to Teresa. They were each other's favorites in the
family and always enjoyed visiting. Unfortunately Teresa lived
several hundred miles from her grandfather and their visits did
not happen as often as she would have liked.

She wasn't certain why, perhaps from being a hospital nurse so
long, but one Autumn Teresa was shaken by an emerging crisis of
faith. She began questioning the existence of her higher power. She
became confused and uncertain about life after death. Prayer and
meditation seemed to be of little help. She decided to consult her
grandfather. Who better to ask than one who has lived a lifetime

and is still happy and content? She planned a visit but was struck with alarm when two days before that date she received a call notifying her of a sudden downturn in her grandfather's condition. She immediately began the six-hour drive, praying all the way that he would be alive. But it was not to be. He slipped away just minutes before her arrival. She stood nearby in tears.

Teresa was used to attending patients during their passing. Most had looks of vacancy or peace on their faces but she had never seen a big smile. Yet here was the most genuine of wide-lipped, happy smiles on the wrinkled and ancient face of her grandfather. She backed away and her tears dried. She felt certain that he was telling her something. She tried to figure it out for some time afterwards but began to understand that reasoning its meaning wasn't important. He had transferred something to her and her faith was once again strong. That's all that really mattered.

X-man

More wordplay, but this got a laugh instead of a boo.

Exvania was a small and isolated country and, except for speaking English, had customs that were often quite unusual. One of these was that the government had an official for each letter of the language. These twenty-six agents were responsible for making sure that their letter was properly represented in any published document and was not frequently abused in poor writing or speaking and especially in profanity.

One of these officials, who was in charge of the letter X, was especially devoted to his work. He loved his letter and was constantly disturbed by the fact that is was used so seldom and almost never in the important position of the beginning of a word. In his effort to improve the visibility of his letter, the X-man came up with a brilliant scheme. In a vigorous campaign he petitioned the government Office of Language to delete the beginning "e" from all words that started with "ex." His rationale was that the "e" was not needed and that neither the pronunciation nor meaning of any word would change. For example "experience" would become "xperience" and "excuse" would become "xcuse," etc. The only effect, he argued, would be a more concise, logical, and modern language. Of course his selfish aim was to get more words to start with his beloved X and especially the biggest prize of all, the country itself, Exvania. It took a huge effort on the part of the X-man but the country was in a slight recession and his figures on the savings in printing ink and paper by the elimination of the "e" were the final argument that made the change official.

You can imagine how this made the E-man feel. He wasn't as fanatically devoted to his letter but was humiliated and became driven with revenge. This revenge finally emerged in a proposal of his own which claimed that all the new words beginning with "x" would surely be understood just as well by eliminating the "x." "We'd all know that perience meant xperience and that ploit meant xploit, etc.," he argued. In addition to revenge, he also had the somewhat selfish motive of having some "x" letters once again begin with "e" such as xercise becoming ercise. The E-man argued his case feverishly and in the end it was actually the X-man's old argument of ink-and-paper-saving that won him the change.

They say that revenge never pays and it didn't in this case. It seems that the E-man had been married and divorced three times. Before all the letter changes took place, he had three ex-wives. That was changed to three xwives. But when his own word change took place, he officially had three wives. That, of course was polygamy and he spent five years in prison for the crime.

Zzzleep

We often talked about our little granddaughter
in New York and this often prompted a story.

His little daughter was finally at the age where she wanted to have books read to her, especially just before she went to sleep. He had awaited this time because he had written several fairy tales during the past year in anticipation. On the first night she requested a story, he read one of his best but was mildly disappointed when she fell asleep before its ending. Undaunted he chose a shorter story the next night but again she was asleep at the end. On the third night, he read his shortest and once again she couldn't quite make it to the end. So he began writing more and shorter stories. But she was falling asleep sooner and sooner every night and just never was awake to hear his endings. This went on and on, shorter and shorter stories and faster and faster to sleep.

One night at a slumber party, when she was an early teen, the girlish talk drifted to the subject of bedtime stories. After listening to her friends talk about their numerous and favorite stories she said with a sigh, "Oh, you girls were so lucky. My dad only knew one story and he read it over and over every night for a couple of years. He read it so many times that I know it by heart. It goes, "Once upon a time there was a beautiful princess who lived happily ever after."

Rosco

*Barbara had so much compassion for many things. She
loved music and had a special empathy for street people.*

Rosco stopped, paused for a moment in reflection, and looked
high to the bright blue spring sky and mumbled "Anything
is possible, everything is possible." These were the words he
remembered from an inspirational book he read over and over
during his last year in prison. Unfortunately his interpretation
was a bit flawed. The book extolled man's capability of reaching
for internal strength for almost any good endeavor, but Rosco
made only the correlation of its message to his profession, crime.
He was thirty years older now and his skills were rusty and the
modern environment unfamiliar.

As he walked the streets of downtown Minneapolis, he noticed
a tattered old man about his age sitting against a building and
holding out a tin cup. And, by gosh, every now and then a passerby dropped a coin in the cup. "What the heck," thought Rosco,
"at least it would be something until I can figure out my next
scam."

And it did work, but even after a whole day the money was
small. Walking the mile back to his little room he again said the
"anything, everything" words. Just then, he noticed a blind man
with dark glasses and a white cane doing just what he had been
doing, but with a lot better luck.

The next day Rosco was implanted at his spot with the equip-
ment of a blind man and a very sad look that he thought was

a nice added touch. Sure enough he doubled his take that day. But a week later he found where the real money was to be made. Walking a different route home he heard saxophone music and found a street player. This guy was really racking in the coin. Rosco played an instrument, a little pan flute that he'd carried around for years. But, no, he was not very good, not even tolerably good. But after another "anything, everything" meditation he was struck with a great idea.

Two days later Rosco sat in his favorite spot with a pan flute to his lips and enchanted music filling the air. A small crowd gathered to listen and most dropped change or even dollars into his cup. "By god," he thought, "I've struck it rich. I'll need a larger cup." What the audience didn't know was that imbedded in the ragged pocket of Rosco's shirt was a cassette player. It was small but expensive and of very good tone. His fellow inmates had given it to him upon his release. His only difficulty had been in finding good pan flute music, which had taken most of the prior day.

Toward the end of the next day, a dignified white-haired gentleman sidled toward Rosco. He waited until they were alone and then spoke to Rosco, looking into the air as if he didn't want to be associated with this bum. "My wife loves pan music," he whispered. "She has all the tapes but has never heard a live performance. It is her birthday tomorrow. I will pay for a new suit of clothes and give you two hundred dollars if you will play for her at a little party tomorrow evening." The gentleman insisted that Rosco be suitably attired and not speak a word. Rosco agreed. He would be picked up by a chauffeur-driven limousine.

The evening was a great success and Rosco received invitations for two more performances. Within a month, he was a minor celebrity amongst the upper class. His rate was now five hundred dollars for an hour, the exact length of his cassette. Then one evening about three months later, before a performance for an elite group of international visitors to the city, the unimaginable happened. Just as he stepped on stage, Rosco discovered that his cassette player was not working. It was too late to turn back. Thinking fast he decided to play a couple of notes and then feign the agony of a cut lip and apologize for not being able to continue. After his introduction and an initial applause the room fell dead silent. Rosco placed his lips on the flute and blew the first long note. "My god," he said to himself, "not bad!" Then came the next note and it was even better. His mind went from thoughts of a cut lip to the third note and then the fourth and fifth. The music was beautiful, enchanting, even better than the cassette. Apparently, all these months, Rosco had been blowing into the flute while mimicking the lip movement and was actually producing music himself. No wonder people told him he was getting better every performance. He had actually been playing with the cassette and his half of the duet was not only improving but surpassing that of the player. Anyway, the performance was so melodic and enchanting that tears came to nearly every eye, including those of Rosco.

Today Rosco is not only famous for being the world's finest pan flute player but noted for his best-selling book titled *Anything is Possible, Everything is Possible.* It's not about his life. It's about his revolutionary method of teaching novices to play musical instruments.

Pickup

We had been talking this day about the line I gave Barbara when we first met. Mine worked better than this guy's.

"What's your card?" he asked the petite girl standing by herself.

"Oh, my gosh," she thought, *"what kind of a pickup line is this."* She'd heard "What's your sign" many times, but never "What's your card." It turned out to be quite refreshing. He explained that since there are fifty-two weeks in a year and fifty-two cards in a deck that he assigned the week of one's birth to one card. January first through the seventh, for example, would be the ace of hearts. This, he elaborated, gives you a whole week to celebrate your birthday instead of just one day.

"Mine is the king of hearts," he said pulling a printed card from his billfold. "Tell me your birthday and I will find yours." She consented and, after probing the card, glowingly pronounced, "Wow! Yours is the queen of diamonds. We're a king and queen!" She laughed and the conversation began. She had planned to be by herself that evening but she enjoyed cleverness, a trait that she sometimes attributed to herself. A friendly and eventually loving evening ensued. She became enthralled and invited him to her apartment for the following night. His pickup line had been successful.

Full of enthusiasm and perhaps even a bit of compassion for her new acquaintance, she browsed through the pages of a calendar the next morning looking up the cards of friends and family, often giggling. Then, in a whim, she rechecked her own card, and checked it again and again. "I'm not the queen of diamonds," she gasped, "not even close. I'm a two of clubs!"

That evening the knock on the door was answered by her roommate. Music and voices could be heard in the background. He introduced himself and asked to come in. "No, no, you can't," replied the roommate. "You must leave. Here, I have a note for you." Wide-eyed, he unfolded the slip of paper and read aloud.

"Sorry, but you cannot join me tonight. You see, I am having a party with Jim and John, who are the seven of spades and seven of hearts, and Ralph and Cory, who are the two of spades and two of diamonds. With my two of clubs, you see . . . well, we already have a 'full house.'"

.

Necktie

A couple of times I had talked to Barbara about starting a business but we decided not to jeopardize the financial security of our family.

This is a true story, claimed the psychic, but you haven't heard it before because it takes place in the future. Not so far into the future that the energy crisis is solved or the world knows peace or things like that, but far enough that fashions and trends have changed considerably. It takes place in a high school auditorium packed with students who came to hear a series of motivational talks by four self-made millionaires. Perhaps the students will get a glimpse of what it takes to make big money after graduation.

But for three hours the talks were a disappointment. The first two speakers had gotten rich playing the stock market for a few years during the 1990s and had pretty much taken it easy ever since. The chances of another boom of such magnitude seemed pretty rare and it sure didn't seem that the speakers' sudden wealth offered much in the way of self-fulfillment. The third millionaire was a real smoothie with a movie-star appearance and a salesman's tongue—that was obviously the way he rose in the ranks of a huge corporation. He was pompous and almost immediately alienated himself from this auditorium of young idealists.

But the fourth millionaire made up for the first part of the program. He was a "regular guy" who came up with the idea of tinting teeth, a fad that he started years ago and that was still a rage. He started making colored dyes in his kitchen and expanded to his garage and then to a small factory. Now half the teenagers in America sport teeth of bright blues, greens, magentas, and reds.

But the part of his story that the students liked most was how he got the idea. He related that it just came to him when he was told an old joke: "A fellow goes to the dentist and complains that his teeth are yellow. 'What can I do?' he asks. The dentist replies, 'Wear a brown tie.'"

During the questions part of the program he was asked how long it took from the time he heard the joke to the time he got rich. "Twenty years," he answered. "During the first ten years I was broke almost all the time." This was a bit of a disappointment until he explained that during those first years he had gotten off to a false start by trying to sell brown ties.

McGowan

*I'm not certain, but maybe so many of these
lifetime stories came about because we were often
talking about life in broad terms.*

John McGowan was born in 1900. On his twenty-first birthday he became an executive in his father's large and hugely successful firm, the Peter A. McGowan Company. John was an independent and perhaps a bit eccentric soul and wasn't crazy about being shoved into the family business. He knew it was his father's dream. What he really wanted was to start his own company. This became a passion in the following years yet he just couldn't figure out what kind of business to start. It frustrated him so much that he finally decided to begin, and hoped that an idea would develop. John bought a new small building on the front of which he placed in large bold letters, "John McGowan Company." He didn't know what type of company it would be but he rationalized that it would surely need a few offices and some vehicles. Trucks, he conjectured, can always be used, so he bought two shiny new Model T's and had "John McGowan Co." painted on their sides.

A year later, bored with being an executive at his father's firm and still having no idea for the nature of his own company, he appeased himself with an expansion, buying two more vehicles. One was a large utility van and the other a heavy-duty flat-bed truck. This made him so happy that he bought two more trucks each year for ten years. He also printed reams of stationery and calling cards boasting "John McGowan Company, John McGowan, Founder and President."

By the time the John McGowan Company celebrated its fifteenth birthday John was a rather wealthy man and, since he was running out of room for his ever increasing fleet of trucks, he decided to expand into a larger building. He bought a few more company pickup trucks and a Mack diesel for any future over-the-road jobs. The company was still without function but he was certain that its growing size would require long-distance rigs.

In 1950 John's father died. Being an only child John inherited everything. With this windfall John became not only the president of his father's business but decided to expand the company that he himself started by building a huge facility with an enormous warehouse for his trucks. The elegant marble-clad main structure contained dozens of offices—all empty, of course. But that would soon change, he told himself. The idea for what his company would produce was bound to come soon. John purposely built on a site that he drove past each day so he could marvel at the huge name, John McGowan, sculpted in stone on his cherished new building.

But the idea never did come, even after sixty years and a few additional trucks each year. On his deathbed, all John could think about was what he'd thought about most of his life: a function for John McGowan Company. In an inspiration he called his favorite nephew and the next day they had a lengthy discussion. John told his nephew that he would leave the company to him if the nephew vowed to keep it intact and, even more important, to find a purpose. "It can be a product or a service company," John emphatically pleaded, "but I want it to be something!" Even if it had to be a reality after his death, he wanted his company operational. His nephew promised and John died a week later.

Within a year, his nephew had fulfilled John's last wishes. The building was not only intact but thriving with business. It still is today and, indeed, is known to some degree around the country. The huge stone name "John McGowan" still emblazes its front with the smaller stone addition below it: "Truck Museum."

Confrontation

I only came home late once without calling Barbara. That was early in our relationship and she still remembers.

His eyes catch the clock. Oh, my god. It's happened again. The guilt is instant. He knows he shouldn't be here. He knows he should have gone straight home. But it's too late now. He kisses her goodbye and hurries out the door. She throws him another kiss and an "I love you." He is too nervous to reply.

The drive home is longer than usual because he has gone out of his way. He will be even later. And this is the second time this week. Even worse he had made a point of telling her this morning that he'd be home on time for a special supper. She will be really mad. And the inevitable questions. He hates those questions. "Well," he thinks in a moment of rationalization, "at least I have made one woman happy."

He is almost home now. From halfway down the block he can see her at the door, hands on hips. Maybe this time he will just blurt out the truth. Yes, he will be honest. And he is. Dropping his bicycle next to the door he exclaims, "I'm sorry, Mom, but I stopped by Grandma's after school and just lost track of time."

L's

*I used to read poetry to Barbara and occasionally
created some especially for her. Yes, even as we got older.*

It was a small poetry reading group of ten people, most in their sixties and seventies. The first gentleman read several works from John Donne and ended on a humorous note with the verses of Ogden Nash that pertained to animals, ending with the one that went something like, "In his wisdom god made fly . . . but what he forgot was to tell us why." The fellow next to him remarked that he knew another Nash animal verse and, indeed, the only one that he himself had set to memory. He recited:

A one "L" lama is a priest,
A two "L" llama is a beast.
But I will bet a silk pajama,
There is not a three "L" lllama.

The group laughed as the lady next to him scratched her head and said, "Maybe there is a three 'L' lllama. How about a big fire?" He got it immediately—a three alarmer—and was extremely impressed. So much so that instead of listening as the readings continued around the table, he silently composed. When it finally came his turn he admitted that he had not come prepared with a contribution but now did in fact have one. It was an addition to the Nash poem on Lamas. He spoke:

Now we must insert a comma,
There is indeed a three "L" lllaama.
It is a blaze of triple trauma,
Now go and find a four "L" llllama

The Compromise

*Barbara was usually adamant about relating her point of
view. On the rare times we argued, a compromise was
preceded by a lengthy debate and often fun conclusion.*

Dad seemed so sure of himself and his ideals. When I was
about ten he agreed that the family could get one pet. My
sister and I were delighted but soon ran into a problem. I wanted
a dog and she wanted a cat. As to our dilemma, Dad stated that
we could get one pet only and if we couldn't decide then he would
suggest a compromise. He loved that word, bragging about some
old guy in history who was called the "Great Compromiser." His
compromise turned out to be one that was unacceptable to both
my sister and me. He said we could either get a dog and she could
pick out the breed, or that we'd get a cat and I'd pick out the breed.
No dice! She would pick out a little cuddly dog that I couldn't
stand and I'd pick out a big mean Siamese cat that she hated. Dad
intervened and said that because we couldn't compromise, he'd
make a decision for us. The next day we had a fishbowl and two
fish. I would rather have had a cat and sis would rather have had
a dog; at least one of us would have been happy. Compromises
didn't seem to make anyone happy.

A couple of months later I heard mom and dad arguing about
getting a new car. Dad wanted a sporty sedan and mom wanted
a station wagon. I burst into the debate and suggested that they
COMPROMISE and get two bikes. Somehow this levity seemed
to affect dad and he backed out of the argument. A week later,

we had a dog, a cat, and a station wagon on order. I was shocked but happy that dad had given up on compromises. He had made three people happy.

That night at the dinner table my dad rather bombastically declared, "Well, I certainly hope this shows us all that a good compromise can make everyone happy." What? Compromise? But he was right about us being happy and for some strange reason he himself seemed the happiest.

Prophecy

Barbara said "I don't get it" when I read her this one.

Many, many years ago there existed a rich and fertile land covered with lush green vegetation and crystal clear lakes and streams. Its people were peaceful and happy under a kind and gentle emperor named Albert Kaye. Albert was a likeable sort, but had the reputation of a playboy. He preferred to "play the field" rather than marry. And although the kingdom was officially one of high religious values, Albert often preferred to nurse a hangover on Sunday mornings in lieu of sitting through long (and what we considered boring) church services. Over a span of many decades of tranquility and personal freedoms this laxity rubbed off a bit on his subjects. At age sixty, Emperor Albert Kaye began to have pangs about this effect and his own legacy. In a desperate attempt to reform he married a young prudish woman of the court named Alice and began to attend church every day. This greatly pleased Alice who was a fanatic about her religion and a zealot for social ethics. In her goal to reform Albert she had much success, except for his martinis at dinner and boilermakers late at night.

One Sunday morning a year later Albert tripped when kneeling, hit his head on the edge of a church pew, and died. It was a very sad occasion for his people who especially feared the changes that might take place now that Empress Alice Kaye was to rule. And changes there were. In her first month she enacted a prohibition against all alcoholic beverages and made Sunday church services mandatory for all subjects, along with dozens of other pious edicts. This enraged the people but because of tradition and love for their kingdom they yielded to her demands. As time went by she became more demanding and even neurotic. She claimed to hear messages from the gods who wished stricter and even more bizarre laws, such as the elimination of kissing.

The people were tolerant until one Sunday morning when she claimed that the gods were angry because all the houses were square or rectangular and nothing else in nature was this shape. "Tear down your houses," she demanded, "and rebuild them as a salute to the vision of the gods in the round shape of their eyes." Enough was enough. Her people revolted, placed her under house arrest, and decided to start a democracy. Then, the next morning during a massive ceremony celebrating her overthrow Empress Alice suddenly appeared on the palace balcony above the crowd and yelled at the top of her voice, "Build your houses in the round or the gods will set them aflame and will make barren the countryside and will cover the land with coldness." They all had a good laugh, passing around the late Albert's secret stash of jugs that they found in the royal stables.

But how things changed! That night every house in the kingdom mysteriously caught fire and burned to the ground. And every tree and plant died and shriveled away. The next day the frightened people ran through some unfamiliar and wildly blowing cold white stuff (later named snow) to reach the palace. They beseeched her majesty to ask the gods for forgiveness. She replied simply, "Build your houses round like the eyes of the gods."

"But the gods have taken our building materials," they pleaded. "Build your houses round," she screamed.

And so they did, and used another unfamiliar material, blocks of ice. Then returning to the palace they told the empress, "All of our houses are round like the eyes of the gods. Even the tops are round! And all of your other wishes, like no kissing, are observed. We only rub noses now. Please, will you ask the gods to bring things back to normal?" The empress was silent. Then a spokesman for the people, one of Albert's old drinking buddies, added an enticement. "Look, your royal majesty," he pleaded, "you tell the gods to reverse things and we'll rename the kingdom after you . . . ah . . . because of your wisdom and greatness and our love for you."

"Very well," she said, sarcastically, knowing a con job when she saw one. So she waited until they officially changed the kingdom's name in her honor. But you know how some women can be when they're pissed off: Empress Alice Kaye never did make the request to the gods.

Charity

*Barbara and I often tried anonymously
to make people happy.*

At age sixty-five, her husband passed away and Charity found herself alone. She sold her house of forty years. It was too big and now too lonely. She was horrified of the thought of being alone and knew she must find a place to live where she could feel a sense of belonging. To her good fortune she finally found an apartment building sponsored by a church that was restricted to seniors. It was a one-story older building but its grounds were beautiful and both its structure and interior immaculately preserved. But what Charity liked most was its strict code of standards. The code assured not only the upkeep of the building but also the proper dress and public language of its residents. The building also had a spacious dining room, a library, and many group activities. Within months Charity felt right at home, and within a year her fellow renters seemed like a new family. She never dreamed that she would be so happy so soon.

Then in her second year, Charity, whose named well described her philanthropy, had a thought that brought joy to her heart. It was the afternoon before Easter Sunday. She would buy nineteen Easter baskets, fill them each with several colored eggs and a large chocolate bunny and place them anonymously by the doors of her fellow tenants. Bursting with happiness in being able to do something good for the people she adored, she enthusiastically finished the task, including delivery, at about 10 PM. But then something strange happened. Perhaps from being around the sweets all day Charity had a sudden sweet tooth attack. Even after a thorough search of the apartment, she could not find a bit of candy. Finally, in desperation, she crept down the hall to the last apartment and removed the chocolate bunny from the bright basket. This same nerve-wracking episode repeated itself until two hours later she had made five separate trips of pilferage. Her sweet tooth finally appeased, she felt very guilty but rationalized that the tenants might guess that the anonymous donor simply ran five bunnies short.

Charity giggled with delight as the buzz about a "phantom" Easter rabbit was a topic amongst hall and lobby talk the next day. But this delight changed on Wednesday in the dining hall when the monthly tenants' meeting was held. The chairman and manager of the building reported some routine business and then dropped a bombshell.

"I have some good news and some very sad news," he said. "The good news is that one of you had the generosity and kindness to leave a beautiful Easter basket at each of our doors on Sunday. This act was in the truest spirit of our group and we thank this mysterious person. However, I hate to report that this deed was somewhat tarnished when someone had the sheer ill-will to actually steal several of the chocolate bunnies from these baskets. At first my only clues as to the culprit was that Mrs. Martin heard footsteps in the hall five times that night and that exactly five baskets were affected. But now things have become clear. Today was garbage day and I felt it my duty to examine the contents of your bags. I'm afraid, Charity, that I found the five chocolate bunny wrappers in your trash. You are our thief!"

Boredom

*I was often prone to boredom but never got bored lying in
bed with Barbara and reading or watching TV.*

In his youth he'd often think about boredom. He was vulnerable when doing tedious chores or doing nothing at all. The only cure seemed to be in indulging in something new or weird. But one thing he learned not to do when bored was to let his dad know, for his dad would immediately come up with some project like mowing the lawn or painting the fence. So when his dad caught him idle he'd say that he was thinking about a school project or that he was tired or sick, but never that he was bored.

One day when he was lazily sitting on the living room sofa peering at a little wooden stature on the mantel and bored stiff, his dad entered the room. Jogging him out of his stupor, Dad asked what he was doing. *Don't tell him you're bored,* he instantly thought to himself.

"Well, Dad, er . . . er . . . er . . . I'm thinking about a story I'm writing for English class."

To his surprise his dad asked him what the story was about. Thinking fast his eye again caught the little wooden statue and he replied, "It's about me . . . er . . . er . . . er . . . when I'm in a lumber yard." He became nervous when his dad asked what he was doing in a lumber yard and a most unusual Freudian slip came involuntarily from his mouth: "I'm getting a little board."

Oh no, he thought, *I'm caught now.* But he wasn't caught. *He's an easier touch than I thought,* he mumbled to himself as his dad shook his head in puzzlement and left the room.

But as it turned out his dad wasn't such an easy touch. An hour later he again entered the room, this time carry a brightly covered box with a bow on top. "This is for you," he said handing it to his son. "It's something you can use the rest of your life."

He carefully unwrapped the package to find a box of a thousand wooden tongue depressors. "What?" he queried.

"Well," stated his dad, "keep one of these with you at all times and you'll never have to get a little board again, not even now while you're mowing the lawn."

The Wise King

*Barbara like stories that momentarily pulled her
thoughts to kings and queens and faraway places.*

Ralphy admired his English teacher——except for one thing that really bugged him. Every couple of weeks the teacher would tell the class to spend the hour writing an impromptu theme and then he'd leave. Ralphy often wondered if it was a hangover, fatigue, or a tryst with another teacher. It was especially annoying since Ralphy had a suspicion that the longest themes, sometimes over five pages, got the best grades. Anyway, it bothered him so much that he devised a plan for the next occasion. When his teacher left the room he began his first page with the title "Preface to my Theme." He continued with a fable of a wise ancient king who had ruled so well that he was convinced to have his biography written. The king put out an edict for Omar, the realm's most renowned writer, to appear at the castle on a certain date.

On that date, not one but two bearded scholarly types showed up at the castle claiming that they were Omar. No one had actually ever seen the genuine writer and this perplexed the men of the king's court. But the king was calm and exclaimed that he would easily find the imposter. He gave both Omars a slate and asked them to write a theme in one hour. One of them began writing immediately and by the time he was finished had filled three slates. The other simply sat and pondered, writing not a word. Everyone felt sure that the real writer had to be the first of the two. But they were stunned when the wise king pointed to the second and in true wisdom stated that "A true writer would spend at least an hour pondering his task before writing even a word."

Ralphy's "Preface" took about a page. On the second page was the bold title "MY THEME" followed by a blank page and ten more blank pages.

The chances of failing or even getting expelled were real, he thought, but it had to be done and he laid it on his teacher's desk with the other themes. But to Ralphy's surprise it was returned two days later with a grade of A. The grade accompanied a note that said, "I don't much care for the "Preface" but the theme itself is a great improvement over your past work."

Wat?son

I was never sure why but every now and then Barbara would delight in musing about how happy the two of us would be together when we grew old.

Mr. Watson, his high school science teacher, was on Joel's "must visit" list this trip home. Joel couldn't help smiling when thinking about this school favorite whose stature was small but whose spirit and mind were huge and always radiated energy and new ideas. Many kids had thought Watson was a bid mad but some, like Joel, luxuriated in offbeat thoughts and mental experimentation. Mr. Watson began most hours by rapidly covering the teachings required by the school board and then spent the rest of class exploring issues like the fourth dimension, infinity, and the nature of time. He dwelled on old enigmas like why a ball can never hit the ground because it must take endless steps of going half way. And he was obsessed with what he called the dual identity of "zero" and "infinity." At other times he'd just relate weird notions such as changing his name from Watson to Wat?son so that it would be unique and he could watch the expressions of hotel clerks who asked him to spell his name. He spent long nights thinking of the nature of things and the kids were the recipient of these thoughts the next day. His lack of sleep was rationalized by, "No snooze is good snooze."

But "time" was Mr. Watson's favorite mystery. He'd tease them with questions like, "If time travels forward and backwards, can it also move sideways?" He insisted that when he retired his major project would be in trying to get time to move backwards, thus he'd become younger.

Joel arrived at the small downtown apartment. A weary, gray-haired old man answered the door. They recognized each other instantly even though it had been twenty years. They visited with enthusiasm in this little room that had space for only a couple of chairs, an old but large TV, and piles of crossword books. Joel became sad when thinking that this once-vibrant communicator was confined to so lonely a place. The good thing was that his beaming mind was well intact.

Joel enjoyed himself as he had in class so many years ago and it was hard to part. Upon leaving he asked, "And, by the way, did you ever figure out how to make time go backwards?"

"No," replied the old man with a wink," but I've sure found how to make it go slower."

Xaoh

Once again a flight from reality.

Isn't it amazing? Just about the time scientists seem to have agreed that Earth has never hosted alien life, a discovery at an archaeological sight in Greece whirls the whole question back on the table. The find was a well-written script from the golden years of Athens. It tells of an alien from a crashed spacecraft that was captured by Pericles himself in 300 BC. According to the document Pericles immediately brought the small metallic-colored creature to the Senate for scrutiny and it was agreed that it must be kept secret so as not to alarm the public. The little alien was indeed a curiosity with a blocklike head and rectangular eyes, three arms, and two very short legs. It seemed inanimate at first until Archimedes noticed a small buttonlike protrusion on its neck. Upon pushing it, the creature's eyes lit up a brilliant blue and it came to life. Aghast, the senators who had been in close examination jumped several feet back.

"Hello," the little being spoke in a monotonic voice, "I am Xaoh."

They all muttered a shy "hello" and waited. But Xaoh did not speak a word until he was asked questions and then the answers were short and direct. Probing inquiries such as "Where do you come from?" and "How did you get here?" were answered with a simple "Question cannot be assimilated."

For hours the senators tried many approaches but got few answers and then only in technical terms, as if coming from the memory bank of a computer. For example, when they asked about his eyes he merely replied "Visual photon receptors" and his mouth was an "intake manifold." They did eventually learn that he was hungry (or as he termed it "fuel deficient") and that the only earthly substance he could assimilate was mineral oil.

After weeks of examination the Senate had learned little about Xaoh and were becoming frustrated. Some of the senators felt that the only way to learn more was to examine his internal workings to find if he was really a living being. If he were a mechanism they might learn much about mechanics from his inner structure. To do this, however, it seemed that they would have to surgically remove the flat leathery plate that was Xaoh's chest cover. Suggesting this to the little alien, however, was met with a quick reply: "Damage Xaoh's chest and Xaoh cease to function forever." This eventually led to a great moral debate. Should they leave him intact and keep him merely as a curiosity or remove the plate and perhaps gain knowledge that might advance the human race. If Xaoh was mechanical everything was fine; but if he was really living with human-type feelings and emotions then it would be murder, which none of them could condone. For days they argued and searched for information from Xaoh, but his constant technical and drone replies seemed only to advance the mechanism theory. If only he could show one sign or even one word of emotion or human frailty, the issue would be dropped. But he did not and the final vote of the Senate was close but weighted to the side in favor of surgery. They agreed that if at any time before the chest plate removal began Xaoh showed the slightest sign of humanity the decision would be reversed. The next day the Senate surgeon was ready to operate.

The ancient script did not say what ultimately happened to Xaoh but it did emphatically state that he was not operated upon and that his chest remained untouched. It seems that at the last minute he showed a single but significant sign of humanity, in fact of quite advanced humanity. As a farewell gesture just before the operation, Pericles had offered him a last flask of mineral oil. In the past Xaoh would have said simply "Thank you" but this time he exclaimed very dramatically, "Pericles, you can take that flask of mineral oil and shove it up your exhaust manifold!"

Heathcliff

It's almost as if we enjoyed poking fun at death.

Bright orange flames engulfed the old mansion and leaped into the air, illuminating the bold marble name HEATHCLIFF carved above the main entry. Water from the hoses of a dozen firefighters disappeared into the structure but had no extinguishing effect. Just behind the firefighters stood the stunned figures of the Heathcliff family, still in their nightclothes, some of which were charred during their narrow escape from the inferno. "At least we are safe," the oldest of the group muttered philosophically. But what was really going through his thoughts was the sudden evaporation of the bitter and long running debate over who would eventually inherit the building from Grandfather Heathcliff. The matter had divided the otherwise loving family into two spiteful sides and now, in what seemed like moments, the ravaging flames deemed the debate finished. They looked at each other with sleepy and doleful eyes.

"Were you able to get to Grandpa Heathcliff on the third floor?" asked a middle-aged woman to the fire chief, as if she already knew his reply.

"Alas, no Ma'am," he answered and the group almost simultaneously bowed their heads to the ground. But heads were not bowed for long as suddenly the youngest of them pointed to the third floor and shrieked, "Grampa! It's Grandpa!" In absolute horror they looked to the inferno and saw Grandfather Heathcliff standing nonchalantly on the third-floor balcony holding a large flaming lamp in one hand and waving with the other. Wide-eyed and in utter shock, they watched as the old man, his nightshirt smoldering, turned and walked back into the billows of orange that folded from the open balcony doors. Two of the women fainted and the others were speechless except for an occasional "Oh my god, oh my god."

The fire chief, who himself was shaken, addressed the group in a pensive voice lamenting, "I am so sorry for you all. To see the old man die in such a terrible way must be horrifying."

After several seconds and in an equally pensive tone the eldest son slowly replied, "We are not horrified by his death tonight. He died peacefully in his sleep three days ago. His body was in a coffin on the third floor awaiting burial on the grounds tomorrow."

Catona

Even though she was sick, Barbara's mind
was ready for word play. Even this sick one.

He spent a lot of time alone, so it was nice to hear the rap at his front door. It was a young fellow bringing a new edition of the Minneapolis phone book. Shucks, he enjoyed older delivery people, especially women, because they tended to take more time to chat. But, what the heck, he enjoyed the courtesy most youth showed toward older folk and he could often catch them off guard with a verbal zinger. This time it was simple: "What? A new book already. I haven't even finished reading the last one!" The kid laughed and so did he. Both of their mornings were made a bit happier.

As he sat in his favorite old stuffed chair, he noticed a large ad for the ballet company on the back of the phone book. The caption read "Come Dance With Me" under which was a photo of a slender ballerina. He closed his eyes and instantly thought of Catona. The thirty years that had passed since meeting her seemed like only moments. In a small nightclub in Portugal, Catona, in a pure white outfit, danced gracefully across a stage whose floor was a brilliant silver. Her grace was amazing; she glided so delicately that her toes hardly seemed to touch ground before they were again in flight. The nightclub act wasn't billed as a ballet, and indeed he had never seen one before, but he knew that this must be what it was like. Since then he had seen many ballets but never with a dancer so felinelike on a shining stage floor. "Oh, Catona," he mused, "I remember you well."

His impression had been so great that he visited Catona backstage after the show and was surprised to find that she was an American from a small town called Williams in Tennessee. She was working her way through a local university. They visited at length and had he not had a loving wife at home he was sure that a relationship would have developed. But it didn't and he never saw her again. He did get her last name, however, just in case. It sounded Dutch, or perhaps Welch: Hottinroof. It didn't seem to go with the romantic Catona. She said that Catona was a stage named she picked to make certain that people would never forget her. "You CAN'T forget Catona Hottinroof, can you?"

Love at First Sight

*Barbara loved romances and
cried easily at romantic movies.*

He had been a groomsman before and doesn't especially enjoy standing motionless in front of a huge church congregation during a long ceremony, especially since he is still a bit tipsy from celebrating the night before. He hopes he can both stay awake and stay standing. Then it happens. His eye catches a vision of beauty in the third row. "My god," he thinks, "I've never seen any one so gorgeous in my life!" He becomes instantly enchanted. "I'm in love!" he says to himself. A moment passes. "Oh my god! she's smiling at me." He smiles back and again she smiles. He feels dizzy, in a stupor. "But, oh no," he suddenly realizes, "she's with another guy." He muses for a moment and squints. "Aha, no ring on her finger, and that guy looks like he might be a cousin or brother. Sure, it's a wedding with relatives. He must be a relative." She smiles again. Three times now; it was more than just casual. "This is a miracle," he thinks. "Sure we're in a church and a divine intervention has happened. I am seeing the girl of my dreams for the first time. Oh, what's she doing now? She's reached into her purse for a pen and paper and is trying to be unnoticed as she writes a note. It's to me! I'm sure its to me." She tips the note toward him and smiles again.

He stands in the reception line eagerly waiting to be free, to seek out his dream girl. Then he notices that she is in the line. She will pass by soon. "She will shake my hand," he said excitedly to himself. "I will touch her skin. And she's carrying something. It's the note! It's the note! Oh lord, let it be for me!"

Her hand is soft and gentle. He almost faints. No words are passed but she does hand him the note. When the last of the guests have passed through the line he scurries to find her but she has gone. No matter, surely her name and number are on the note. He squeezes the note tenderly and puts it in his pocket. He will savor it like unopened Christmas presents when he was a kid. He will take it home and open it in a serene moment by his fireplace when he's alone. And this he does, cleaning the living room, putting on a comfortable robe, dimming the lights, and playing soft romantic music.

Settling into a big comfortable chair he relaxes for several minutes and then murmurs, "Well, here goes." He invokes visions of his dream girl's lovely face, gently kisses the note, slowly unfolds it, and reads: "Your fly is open."

Mom

*These short stories weren't meant to be bedtime stories but
Barbara was in bed and sometimes they felt that way.*

He was almost twelve years old, but he still enjoyed his father's
bedtime stories about his grandma. He'd heard this one
before but that didn't matter. His dad closes his eyes and begins.

One of my favorite memories of Mom was the walks along
the country road we'd take when I was a boy. I didn't enjoy them
at first but she lured me into creating little games that we played
along the way. The one I liked most was when one of us was the
"pessimist" and the other the "optimist." We'd note things on the
landscape and the pessimist had to make a downbeat observation. The optimist would then have to change that negative view
into a positive one. One late fall trip I was the "pessimist" and
pointed to the leaves falling from trees and commented that trees
must be really dumb because they were shedding their clothes
just as winter was approaching. She retorted that they were not
dumb but compassionate because they were offering their clothes
to the cold ground. At bit farther down the road we passed the
old abandoned farmhouse and barn. I said that they looked like
dead things that somebody had forgotten to bury. "Oh no," she
responded, "they are no longer things at all. They are now memories and it would be a true shame to bury what are probably wonderful memories." She was always so quick with her comebacks
when she was the optimist. I guess it just came naturally.

On the walk back I noticed Uncle Dave's car in the driveway.

This excited me because he was kind of wild and would tell crude jokes and stories that always had Mom saying, "Not in front of the kids, Dave!"

Completely forgetting the game I jumped up and yelled, "Hey Mom, look, Uncle Dave is here."

"Oh," she snapped back, "well, maybe he won't stay long."

Fear of Flying

Barbara loved to fly and so did I until I got older.
She always showed empathy.

She was somewhat bitter that she didn't get the job, but at least some good had come of it. During her interview with the personnel manager she had offhandedly mentioned that she had completely solved her fear of flying problem in one day. The company had seen this problem in some of its executives and he suggested a one-time return visit by her to give a talk to a select group of sufferers. They agreed on $2,000 plus expenses and here she was in a plush conference room at the podium.

She began by relating her initial enjoyment of flying but then described how an insidious fear infected her like a cancer and grew more intense every year until she became desperate. She read books and enrolled in classes, but nothing worked. She had tried heavy doses of alcohol before flights, but this only made her senses more acute and the fear worse. She even experimented with knockout drugs, but they proved unreliable when twice she had to be carried unconscious on a stretcher off the plane. And in a bizarre effort she paid $200 for a pair of glasses that made everything appear nearer; the theory being that when looking out the window the ground would seem very close. Her last and final attempt, and the one that solved her problem, was recommended by a retired pilot who noticed her anxiety in an airport lobby. He conjectured that if she flew in the back seat of a stunt plane for a half hour that her fear would be literally "scared" out of her and that a commercial flight would then seem no more risky than riding in a bus. It took a lot of nerve but she was desperate and they arranged the test.

"It was by far the most frightening incident in my life," she explained, "but it worked. It solved my problem and I haven't been afraid of flying since." An anxious participant asked if she thought her method would work for everyone. She gave her reply as she checked her watch and picked up her brief case. "No," she said, "not if you must do a lot of flying. You see, it solved my problem by scaring me so much that I vowed to god that if I got back safe I'd never fly again. So now, no flying, thus no fear of flying. Thank you, gentlemen," she said as she walked out the door, "but I have a train to catch."

Be Careful

This story is true. Barbara was there and loved it.

"Can I look inside your new van, Lee?" piped the squeaky-voiced little six-year-old. Lee and his dad were drinking coffee at the kitchen table. In the driveway sat a sparkling new black van that was elaborately furnished with all the latest electronic bells and whistles. Not only did it have standard features but a host of custom accessories that made its interior resemble the cockpit of an airliner. With a touch of a button, knob, or lever, you could not only raise windows and dual antennae but lift the hood, elevate the rear end, expose flood lights, and lower visors. And this was just for starters.

"Why, what the heck. Sure you can, if it's okay with your dad," Lee said, smiling. The boy turned eagerly to his dad who thought for a moment, then agreed, but in a louder than normal voice cautioned, "but Be Careful!"

Handing him a key ring containing a button-laden plastic fob Lee said, "Just push this green button and the side door will open for you." His eyes beaming, the boy took the fob and rushed out the door. Shortly the men heard the deep swish of the van door opening.

A few minutes later it was the kitchen door that opened and before the two men stood the same little boy, but the glowing face had been replaced by one of sheepishness and perplexity. Lowering his head a bit and raising his eyes to his dad he timidly asked, "Be careful of what?"

Short

Barbara and I were the same height, 5' 6", but she just looked taller. I regularly made jokes about me being short.

Dinner was ending when one of his ten-year-old twins asked the father, "Do you think Tommy and I will be tall or short like you when we grow up?"

The father chuckled and replied, "Well, I sure hope you won't be tall." When asked to explain, the father elaborated: "Shorter men are just better for the world. Their clothes and shoes take less material. They eat less, pollute less, and breathe less of our precious oxygen. If all men were short we'd have smaller beds, cars, highways, and just about everything else. And what's more, statistics show that shorter men are healthier, work harder, earn more money, and live longer. In short, pardon the pun," he smiled, "they are just more efficient machines."

"Are tall men better at anything?" the twins asked. The father thought for a moment and then admitted, "I guess you might say they are a little better at attracting women."

As they left the table the father asked, "You two want to grow up to be short, don't you?"

Without hesitation and in unison the twins retorted, "Nope."

Simon

I rarely got mad about anything. But when I did I can remember Barbara asking, "Is that what you are really mad about?" How did she know?

He was delighted but surprised when Simon asked him to sit in on his weekly card party. They had been friends for some time but Simon's crowd was at least a couple notches above him in social class and wealth. What he wasn't surprised at was the low poker stakes. But maybe being a tightwad was one key to Simon's success.

The Victorian house was neat but furnished opulently. He was the last to arrive and, apologizing to the six gentlemen in the parlor, quickly removed his coat. But it was a bit too quickly, catching on his shoulder and swooping up to knock over a large ceramic vase. He jumped back in horror at the three large pieces on the floor.

Simon jolted from his seat, ran to where the vase had fallen and threw his arms in the air. Then with a rage that seemed very unlike his friend he screamed, "What in the hell have you done? I just bought this vase! You clumsy oaf! Why didn't you take your coat off in the hall like the rest of us? You idiot!" and on and on.

He tried to apologize but couldn't be heard over the ranting of Simon. Finally, in a bit of disgust himself, he grabbed his host by the shoulders and shouted, "Look here, Simon! It was an accident and I'm truly sorry! I don't have a lot of money but I'll gladly pay for it!"

Instantly Simon lowered his arms, dropped his head, and in a soft and almost sheepish voice said, "No, I couldn't let you do that."

"But the vase obviously meant a lot to you. I must at least pay for it," he insisted.

"No, I couldn't let you do that. I just couldn't let you do that," repeated Simon.

"But, Simon, I will. I must," he urged.

Simon looked him in the eyes and in a stern voice replied, "You just don't understand. It was not your breaking the vase that upset me. It was that I knew I couldn't let you pay for it."

Wishes

Sometimes both Barbara and I wanted to distort reality.

A taxi, exhausted by its tedious job, was parked at the zoo next to a fence behind which stood a very bored elephant. The taxi and the elephant were lamenting their circumstances when a genie suddenly appeared and offered to grant them a wish. After considerable thought, they decided that life would be much better for both if they exchanged trunks. The taxi could then work for the fire department, racing to blazes and using its new trunk to spray water. That would be very exciting. And the elephant could pick up visitors in his spacious new trunk and give them thrilling rides. And he could suck up more than peanuts, perhaps sandwiches and hotdogs. The two were ecstatic with their decision. Warning them that once made the change was permanent, the genie went "poof" and the deed was done.

The taxi drove off, very happy with its long gray appendage, at least for a while. Then one day speeding to a brush fire he had to stop for gas. The attendant, who was not very bright, mistakenly pumped gasoline into the cylindrical trunk. Arriving at the small fire he planned to extinguish in one great squirt, he let go with a powerful thrust. It took five large fire trucks to put out the resulting inferno. He was dismissed from the department and wandered sadly back to the zoo. Here he found his trading partner also in a state of despondency. On the fence was a sign that said not "elephant" but "trashephant." It seems the zookeeper found that the best job for this strange-looking beast with the large square trunk was to pick up trash and haul it to the dump.

Again the taxi and the elephant lamented and again the genie appeared. They beseeched her to reverse their conditions, but she was helpless. It was one of those genie laws. But she did declare that one final wish could be granted. After a great deal of discussion, they told her that since they couldn't exchange trunks again that they wanted everything but their trunks switched. Pretty tricky, thought the genie, but nevertheless she "poofed," and it was done.

The elephant, who now looked like a taxi, was overjoyed with its new high-paced occupation. And the taxi, now an elephant, was delighted to be off the busy streets and in the peaceful environs on the zoo. Consider this the next time you catch a cab and find a few peanuts in the back seat.

The Tortoise and the Hare

Opposing perspectives always entertained Barbara.

"Tell me a story, Grandpa," Timmy stalled for time when being tucked into bed. This grandpa, a retired chief accountant, was proper and stoic and the story would probably be boring, but at least it would delay turning out the lights.

Grandpa agreed and proceeded with the old tale of the race between the tortoise and the hare where the tortoise's slow but determined pace won because the cocky and confident hare played and dallied and finally fell asleep against a tree. "The moral of this story," he told the now yawning boy, "is that if you set goals in life and steadily attend those goals without deviation you will eventually be successful. This was the key to my success." Grandpa turned off the lights and Timmy fell asleep.

A few weeks later Timmy spent the night at his other grandpa's house and again asked for a story. This one would probably be more exciting because the second old man was quite flamboyant. He had been a successful salesman and business owner. Grandpa number two had actually employed Grandpa number one for many years and they both retired quite wealthy.

"Hmmm," he pondered, rubbing his chin, "how about the story of the race between the turtle and the rabbit?" Timmy asked if it was anything like that of the tortoise and the hare. "Oh, no," he replied, "very different."

Timmy agreed and the story began. It involved a rabbit who convinced a turtle to join him in staging a phony race where the rabbit would intentionally lose. Before the race began, the two took bets on the underdog turtle whose odds were officially set at one in one hundred.

The race began and the rabbit had a ball gallivanting and then daydreaming while resting, not sleeping, under that tree. The plodding turtle went on to cross the finish line and they both became wealthy. Timmy wasn't yawning this time and anxiously asked about the meaning of this version.

"The moral of this story," stated Grandpa number two, "is that if you link up with a determined and unwavering partner in this life you can have one heck of a lot of fun yourself and you both will eventually be winners."

Quarters

Barbara loved her children dearly and
always enjoyed stories about young people.

They had finished Mr. Houser's yard work and sat at the picnic table waiting to be paid. Finally the old man emerged from the house and smacked two shiny new quarters on the table. The two smiled at each other but upon Houser's departure the older boy, Ralph, snatched up both coins, stashing them in his back pocket, and ran across the yard toward home. Johnny, who was often abused by his older brother, jumped up and chased after him, screaming. Ralph probably would have gotten away with this petty theft, but while looking back to check his lead he ran smack into Dad. "Whoa, whoa," exclaimed his father. "What's going on here?" Ralph was paralyzed. The thought of his dad catching him stealing and exacting a painful punishment put terror in his little body. Johnny approached, panting from the run, yelling, "He stole my quarter, Dad! He stole my quarter! It's right there in his back pocket."

In a stern and frightening voice, Dad peered at Ralph and asked him if Johnny was telling the truth. Ralph knew that he should admit to it or maybe claim it was an accident and hope for leniency, but he froze in fright and what came from his trembling lips was, "No, Dad." Now, he not only stole but he lied! Oh how he hoped that dad wouldn't check his pocket.

But no luck. The big man stooped down to Ralph, his giant

hand dwarfing the little pocket, unable to make a search. "Darn," he scowled and pointed to the younger boy. "You check."

Johnny anxiously scoured the pocket. Ralph cringed in anticipation but after what seemed to be more than enough time Johnny's hand suddenly and rapidly exited the pocket. "Oops." He immediately looked up to his dad, "I guess I was wrong. He must not have taken it after all."

Dad stood up, firmly warned Johnny to be cautious about his accusations, and walked away.

In a state of astonishment, Ralph walked into the house and sat down on the couch. His sense of relief was such that he didn't even think about the money. He was just happy to be unscathed.

And Johnny was happy too. He did get a mild reprimand, but what the heck, he was able to get his big brother out of trouble and he did have two quarters.

One Line

This was one of Barbara's favorites.
She laughed and laughed.

If he knew how much most of his students loathed his little
math puzzles he probably wouldn't put them to the torture so
often. But he loved games and reveled in testing teenage minds.
Yet this morning they'd be spared because he had been forced to
bring his four-year-old son with him to class when his sitter was
called away. Maybe he'd have them do paperwork while he spent
time with the quiet little boy whose legs dangled from a chair in
the back of the room.

But the opposite was true and in unusual pomp he began
with a quiz. Perhaps he was attempting to impress his son with
mathematical prowess. With a gleam in his eyes, he drew several
rows of dots on the blackboard and told the class, "I want you to
tell me the least number of straight lines it would take to connect
each of these dots. The only qualification is that no line can cross
another. You have five minutes." Some quickly going to work and
others yawning reluctantly, the students copied the maze of dots
and began drawing and erasing lines.

"Time's up," he soon pronounced. "Now, how many of
you have six or more lines?" One lazy hand rose. He smiled.
"How many have five lines." Most of the remaining hands
rose. Again he smiled. "And how many have four lines?" Two
hands snapped up. He looked disappointed, as if hoping no
one would answer correctly. As he glowingly began explaining

every logical detail of the solution a squeaky voice piped from the back of the room.

"But Dad, that's wrong 'cause it can be done with only one line." A bit embarrassed, the teacher asked the little boy to just sit and listen. He continued with the explanation. When the bell rang and students were gone, he bent to his son and in a kindly voice explained, "I didn't want to stop you, Albert, but you must not have been listening when I said that the lines had to be straight."

"But I was listening, Dad. My one line was straight. It was just a very thick line."

Exercise

*I told Barbara that this story was true, then admitted
that it wasn't. She smiled and said, "I know."*

He was a good teacher and loved experiments, especially
since the class now had computers. On this morning he had
brought in a television set and explained an experiment he called
"Exercise." He placed a black cloth over the screen and played a
ten-minute video of an outspoken character named Jed who was
pleading his minor lawsuit in family court. When it was complete
he asked us to bring up a program on our computers that he
had designed the previous night. On our screen was the outline
of a man's figure. "This is Jed," he explained. "He is an outline
now but each of you will turn him into a real person based on
what you've heard from the TV." In a corner of the screen were
dozens of printed categories with options such as type and color
of clothes, facial characteristics, hair style, and even body height
and size. By clicking any option button, Jed was immediately
endowed with that feature. By the end of the exercise, we all had
our Jeds, each one unique. One was a jeans-clad stocky Jed with a
mustache while another was a slender Jed, balding and wearing a
dark green suit. We made prints of our creations and the teacher
pinned them on the wall.

"The purpose of this experiment is to show that when we
watch television we use no imagination," he enthusiastically proclaimed. "But when we black out the picture, we are forced to
use our individual imaginations." He pointed to our creations on

the wall. "We essentially exercise our creativity. Just as we exercise our bodies in the gym, we now exercise our minds. And my guess is that just as our bodies improve from exercise so will our minds." I don't think he expected any of us to actually watch TV without a picture in the future but it did set us to thinking about his supposition.

A few months later I had to take a physical for entry into graduate school. One of the questions on the medical form asked how often I exercised. I was about to check the "never" box but then stopped and marked the one that said "regularly." I didn't feel this was false. After all, I did listen to my car radio every day when driving to classes.

The Inventor

"Don't you dare!" she told me.

On their way to the hospital a boy and his friend stopped by the old man's little house to pick up some things he'd requested. The friend was amazed to see three walls of the tiny living room covered with plastic framed patent certificates. There were hundreds of them. "Are these all your Grandpa's?" he inquired. The boy related that his grandpa was an avid inventor. When asked if his grandpa was rich the boy chuckled and told him that the old man barely made enough to pay for patent applications. It seems that each invention was just a bit over the edge in terms of practicality.

"Let me show you," he said, examining the wall. "Ah, here are a few on tires." The first one was a concept that would switch rubber tires and concrete roads to concrete tires and rubber roads; the advantage being that rubber trees would be planted along the highway and repaving would be a simple matter of tapping the trees. The patent next to it was for tires impregnated with a scent so that as they slowly wore out on the highway the traces of material evaporating into the air would impart a fresh pine scent to the countryside. They both chuckled.

Grandpa would be in the hospital for a week and he had asked the boy to bring his patent files, some shaving gear, and his sack of lollipops. The grandson felt sad that the genial old man couldn't indulge in his pipe and the nips of vodka that he so relished at home. But he felt better when his grandpa responded to a suggestion he made upon returning to the hospital. "They'd smell your pipe in here, Grandpa, but I sure could smuggle in a little bottle of vodka," he offered.

"Thanks, but no need," the twinkle-eyed old man said, smiling. He pulled a transparent lollipop from the paper bag and pointed it at him, "Patent number four hundred and seventy-one."

Love

*One thing that was never in question was our deep love
for each other. In those last months we said
"I love you" several times every hour.*

Now it was real, a genuine affair, she thought nervously
entering the hotel room. He, too, was nervous so they just
sat at the side of the king-size bed for a few moments, arms around
each other's shoulders. She wasn't so much hesitant because of
cheating on her husband; he had been cheating on her for years.
Her concern was the question of whether this affair was really
love or just fascination or some distorted means of revenge. She
had always prided herself on being a highly moral person and it
was of extreme importance that this was true love. But now at
this late moment she just wasn't sure.

They rather formally changed into nightwear and carefully
began fondling one another in a prelude to a romantic and sen-
suous night. Suddenly they heard music from the adjacent room
just behind the wall near their bed. It wasn't deafening but just
loud enough to be a distraction. They tried to ignore it but it was
no use. Frustrated he jumped up, put on a long robe, and left the
room saying he'd back in a moment.

Five minutes went by, then ten, then twenty. She had heard
him knock on the neighboring door but the music hadn't stopped
and he hadn't returned. When half an hour passed, she donned
her robe and reluctantly made her way to the room next door.
About to knock she noticed that the door was ajar and ever so

cautiously she eased it open. The room was eerie and dark except for two flickering candles and an old phonograph that was now playing "Mack the Knife."

"Rudy?" her now frightened voice called. "Rudy. Rudy, are you there?" Suddenly from behind a bedroom door next to one of the ghostly candles came a faint but shrill, "Help me! Help me!" Terrified, she instantly bolted back to her room. In seconds she was dressed and racing down the hallway to the elevators. On the main floor she ran past the front desk and out into a taxi that had just pulled up. As it drove off into the night, she finally relaxed. Rubbing her forehead in relief she said quietly to herself, "Well, I guess it wasn't really love."

Apples

*Sometimes after stories about kids, Barbara would laugh
and say "Doesn't that remind you of one of our kids?"*

He took the shortcut to town through the woods. No need to rush, though. The carnival would be opening soon but he had no money. This bothered him immensely and he stopped to rest under an old apple tree. Gazing up at the fruit-laden branches, his thoughts ricocheted between ways to make money and bitterness toward his dad who had refused to give him any. As if these two thoughts had suddenly collided, he had a brainstorm. Without hesitation he pulled off his sweater, tied a knot at the end of each sleeve, and began climbing the tree. In no time he was back on the ground with a sweater full of bright red apples. He polished one on his pants and bit into its crisp and succulent flesh. It was delicious.

It took him only an hour to peddle his fruity stash outside the carnival gate. At a dime an apple he had nearly four dollars, plenty enough for a great afternoon.

Later in the day he walked home with an Elvis banner and a small blue teddy bear under his arm. "Where you been?" asked his dad who was washing the car in the driveway. He held out his mementoes and enthusiastically replied that he'd been at the carnival. "But who gave you the money?" his dad snapped back.

"Well, Dad," he grinned, "in a way you did."

"But I refused to give you any," said Dad. "You'd already spent your allowance."

"I know, Dad, but I was so mad at you that I walked to town anyway and on the way I came up with the idea of picking apples from that old tree in the woods and selling them in town."

"That's just great," his dad stated proudly, "but what did I have to do with it?"

"Well, I got the idea when I was looking up at the tree and cursing your last words. Remember? You said, 'Money doesn't grow on trees.' Guess you were wrong this time, eh, Dad?"

Thog

And another escape from reality.

"This is the story of the greatest Neanderthal who ever lived," announced the young new minister to his first Sunday school class. "His name was Thog. He not only created many of man's most important inventions but saved the last group of these ancient people from certain extinction." Not too bad for a church story, thought the kids, and they listened attentively. It seems that Thog had first invented what he called the "wheel" and when it replaced the "squares" on carts, the ride was much smoother. This was followed by many other inventions, such as the hot dog and the boomerang. One morning Thog told the villagers that he had completed his greatest invention and would demonstrate it later that day. It was, he claimed, the best thing since sliced bread, which he had developed a few years earlier.

That afternoon he wheeled a huge barrel of liquid to the center of the little village where everyone had gathered. Excitement abounded as he exclaimed, "This is a new beverage, better than water and tastier than milk. I call it 'beer.'" The townspeople were hesitant at first but soon joined Thog in enthusiastic indulgence. Everyone became happy and acted delightfully strange. The glee and dancing lasted late into the night. The men praised Thog and insisted that he immediately chisel the recipe for this "beer" on the face of a big stone, lest it ever be forgotten.

The next morning was quite different. They awoke in torment, suffering as never before, with headaches and dizziness. In utter disgust a group of the strongest men, now reduced to glassy-eyed, vomiting slugs, pushed the large rock on which Thog had chiseled his recipe over a cliff where it bounced wildly for miles to the valley below. Thog sadly walked away, never to be seen again. One week later several huge boulders fell from the mountain above, demolishing the village. "End of story," said the minister.

What? thought the kids. Is this about the evils of drink? Had God killed them? "But wait. Hold on a minute," they asked. "You said Thog saved them."

"Oh, yes, in a way he actually did," replied the minister. "You see, nobody was hurt. They were all down in the valley looking for the recipe."

Word to the Wise

Sometimes I teased Barbara by
playing with her favorite little truisms.

Memories abounded as he entered the old brick building. Thirty years had passed since his grade school days but the school hadn't really changed. Glancing into the first room he could almost hear the crackling voice of Mr. Johnson who had so often sent him to the cloakroom for misbehaving. And, oh yes, little Lydia whom he tried to impress by getting into even more trouble. He hadn't taken school seriously in those first few years. He hadn't understood that school was something other than a social gathering.

Across the hall was the office of the principle, Mrs. McGinty. A shiver passed through him. He had had many run-ins with her, but none worse than the day when he was called into her office to find his mother with an uncommonly solemn look on her face. They wanted to set him back a grade. This would have put him in his younger sister's class, an unfathomable horror to a ten-year-old boy. His pleading and tears finally convinced them to give him a second chance. This event changed his grade school life. He was instantly transformed from the school clown to its most serious and hardworking student.

Farther down the hall was the room of Mrs. Olson, the fifth grade teacher who had so diligently facilitated his transformation. This kindly woman had taught him to grasp the meaning of his subjects, and school soon became a place of enjoyable learning.

Yes, she was his favorite and he especially recalled the adage that she quoted aloud as the class filed out the door at the end of the day: "A word to the wise is sufficient." Every day, "A word to the wise is sufficient."

Continuing the nostalgic tour he paused in the empty gymnasium where four long braided ropes still hung from the ceiling. He had been the school climbing champion, his first and only athletic accolade. Through the window he saw the old playground, now overrun with weeds and debris. "Recess," he thought, "the true meaning of school up until the fifth grade."

After another hour of living in his past he walked back through the ancient front door to his car. Suddenly he stopped. A strange thought entered his mind. If "*a word* to the wise is sufficient," then why had Mrs. Olson felt she had to tell them these words *every* day? It wasn't until he'd driven down the street that he realized her wisdom.

Emotions

It has always amazed me how happy Barbara and I were almost all of the time. We were very rarely sad or gloomy.

She sat motionless on the park bench, a forlorn gaze cast into the bright spring sky. His smile did not distract her oblivion so he sat down. "Nice day," he offered.

"Perhaps," she replied softly.

"You look so desolate," he said with concern. "Did I catch you in the middle of a deep thought?"

"No, I am not thinking. I'm just sad."

"I'm so sorry," he said. "Did something bad happen?"

"No, nothing bad."

"But you just look so . . . well . . . I guess lonely or in grief," he probed.

She turned, catching his eyes, "Look, I am not lonely, not in grief, not ailing, not reminiscing, not poor, not unhealthy, not anything except sad. Just sad. Very sad."

"Can I do anything to help?"

Peering into the sky, she answered his question with one of her own. "Are you happy?"

"Yes, yes I am," he replied rather giddily.

"Why are you happy?" she snapped back.

"I guess I don't really know why," he said after a moment's thought. "Maybe it's the beautiful morning, the bright sun, the fresh air, or just that I feel good. I don't really know."

Again she turned to him, this time with glaring eyes and a

bitter tone. "Well I don't know why I'm sad either so why don't you just go and be happy on another bench and let me be sad on this one?"

Instantly he stood and walked off, not quite as happy as he'd been moments before. She continued her blank gaze but perhaps not quite as sadly as before.

Office #1

Before we were married, Barbara worked in an office.
One of her old co-workers visited, making her very happy.
Office stories were fun for several days.

It was difficult to keep from laughing as I watched the managers file into the conference room. They looked like pompous penguins, especially my own manager, Bob Kessler, the worst of the lot. But I had fixed them good this time. They were going to a meeting that wasn't a meeting. The memo I sent them wasn't signed. It just said "Meeting–10 AM in conference room. Please be prompt." The door closed and I chuckled in anticipation for them to file right out. But they didn't file right out. An hour passed and then another before the door finally opened and they all walked, quite happy.

The next day, to my astonishment, I found out what had happened. It seems that the meeting went so well that they made plans to make it a weekly event. And what's even worse is that Bob Kessler took credit for calling the meeting. That damn Kessler! That meeting wasn't his idea. It was mine! He stole my idea! Well, I wasn't going to stand for that so I spread the rumor that I was the instigator of the meeting.

The rumor mill must have worked pretty well because the next day Bob Kessler called me to his office and fired me. He said that the meeting had taken so long because they had to develop a plan to catch the culprit. "It was my plan that we decided to go with," he stated arrogantly.

That damn Kessler!

Office #2

I argued at length. "It was just one little mistake, one little decimal point error entered into the computer," I insisted. Sure, it changed the invoice price of the new product from fifty dollars to five dollars but my part was just one little slip. And it was just sheer bad luck that no one caught it until eighty thousand units were sold. "It was simply human error," I exhorted.

But it was to no avail. My boss replied that the company had no room for human error. I was fired.

But I learned later that the company did have room for human error. You see, before I left I moved the decimal point in the opposite direction on the program that prints all the company rebate checks. It was quite costly for the company but they didn't fire my boss. "Why would they fire him?" you ask. That's simple. He made a human error. He fired me.

Office #3

He often wondered how anyone could have the gall to refer to those little cubicles as offices. Even animals in the zoo weren't confined to such small quarters any more, he thought. And what's worse is that the six-foot plastic walls seemed to get a little closer together every year. But he had tolerated twenty years here and guessed he could struggle through another twenty. Oh, this wasn't his original plan. Not at all. He once had grand plans of moving to California and finding a job where he could work outdoors. This was going to be a temporary job to gather a nest egg. He hadn't planned on meeting his wife and having a child so soon. Then the money became more important. He wasn't much of a risk taker and the original plans gradually transposed themselves into daydreams that he knew would never come true.

It was ten o'clock and time for his ritual walk to the coffee machine. He passed Bill Orten who, as long as he could remember, spent his breaks staring aimlessly out the large glass window at the end of the hall. "I guess it could be worse," he thought, "I could be old Bill. He's been here forever and always looks so haggard and so sad, every break and most of the lunch hour just peering forlornly out of that window. What does he see? Does he count cars or is there a pretty girl in the office across the street?"

He'd rarely spoken to Bill but his curiosity was now roused. They exchanged "hellos" and then there was a long pause after which he asked if there was anything in particular that Bill looked at so faithfully. Bill nodded without breaking his gaze. "Do you mind if I ask what it is?" he inquired.

In a soft voice came the one-word answer. "Freedom."

Two weeks later, he was in California.

Office #4

The interview had gone well and now the applicant listened attentively to the graying man whose job he aspired to fill.

"Ken," he said, "I like you and you have the experience and skills to fill my job, but since you're primarily money motivated I will give you some confidential advice. The job you want is not with us but with our competitor." Ken looked genuinely perplexed. "Let me explain with a story," continued the older gentleman. "I started with our company many years ago as sales manager for its weakest territory. Devoting myself to the job I built that territory, the one you're applying for, into the largest and most profitable in the company. Then one day I got a shock from our president, the old goat. He had changed the bonus program from being based on sales to being based only on sales increases. You see, Ken, I had my territory optimized with almost no room for further growth. I had very little opportunity for a bonus and I let the old geezer know my feelings. But he wouldn't yield. He said that the future of the company was in growth and that's where our incentives should be placed. I asked for another less saturated territory, but he insisted I stay where I was known and liked. It was a stalemate, and in an impulsive move, I quit and went to work for our competitor, servicing the same territory I had left. I didn't much care for their product or reputation but they had a bonus program based on sales increases and I knew I could make a killing. And I did make a killing, increasing sales dramatically every year for five years. I was thinking of retiring early but I got a call from the president here and he made me an offer to return that I just couldn't refuse. Bonuses were still based on sales increases but that was fine then because the territory had lost half its prior customers.

"That was five years ago. I made another killing and now the territory is once again optimized. So, Ken, your best move is to apply for the position open with our competitor. I know some tricks that will make it a cinch for you. And with me gone from here you should be able to make your own killing." Ken thanked him profusely and left. The president stopped by the interviewer's office and asked how things went.

"Great," he replied. "He's a terrible salesman and I'm sure he'll get the job."

Bluff

Another "Doesn't that remind you of . . . "

The words between little Johnny and his mother were short and terse.

"Why doesn't Jenny have to do any work? Why can she watch TV and I have to clean up?"

"Because Jenny's room is clean and Jenny helped me with the wash while you were playing with your friends!"

"You just like Jenny better than me. You hate me!"

"If that's what you think, young man, then you can just go to your room for the night!"

"I'll go to my room, Mom! I'll go to my room and pack! I'm leaving this place! That should make you and Jenny both happy! He ran to his room and slammed the door.

Shaking her head she walked down stairs and called for her husband who was doing crossword puzzles on the couch. "What do I do now, Harold?" she exclaimed. "He says he's going to run away from home. I'm tempted to lock him in his room."

"No, dear, don't do that," replied Harold calmly. "I'll take care of things."

Johnny, suitcase in hand, met his dad as he was walking out the front door. The words between them were short and terse.

"Where ya goin', son?"

"I'm runnin' away from home and never comin' back!"

"In that case I'll lock this door and never let you come back."
A long pause.

"Are you bluffin', Dad?"

"Ya. Are you bluffing, Johnny?" Another long pause.

"Ya."

"How long do you expect to be gone?" A short pause.

"I supppose about a hour or two."

"I'll leave the door open."

Liar

Boy, did I get into trouble if I told Barbara even a little lie.

Dad could be accused of a lot of things but being a liar wasn't one of them. Over the years he smoked, drank, cheated, and gambled but he prided himself on never having lied. That is until one evening during a conversation with my brother Ned, who had incidentally picked up none of dad's bad habits except gambling, at which he was quite proficient.

The two had played poker for several hours with winnings switching back and forth When they were about to call it a night each found themselves looking at a great hand. After several bets and raises, Ned, not revealing his hand, jokingly asked Dad if he could beat a natural full house. In equal jest Dad said, "Sure." Ned smiled confidently and said, " In that case we should bet the works," shoving all his chips to the center of the table. "Fine," said Dad, who did likewise. Jubilantly Ned slapped down a full house upon which Dad immediately revealed his winning straight flush. "Damn!" shouted Ned. The loss didn't bother him so much as the oration that followed. "You should have known better," Dad exclaimed. "I told you that I had you beat and I've never ever told you a lie. Never, son, never! You should have listened."

He rambled on until Ned could take no more. He interrupted, declaring firmly, "Dad, you have lied to me!" This started a debate that ended with an indignant dad offering to wager his entire poker winnings that Ned could not cite one occasion where he had lied to him. Ned accepted, looked Dad squarely in the eye, and said just two words, "Santa Claus." Dad instantly knew that he was beaten, that years ago he had told Ned that there was a Santa Claus.

But Ned, like Dad, was ruthless and wouldn't relent. "I'll tell you what, Dad, I'll give you a chance to win the money back. I'll bet you that you've lied to me twice."

Dad didn't have to think very long. He knew that he hadn't made claims about the Easter Bunny or Great Pumpkin and other than that had always been very careful to tell the truth. He agreed and eagerly awaited Ned's reply.

With an air of cockiness Ned rose from the table. "Just write me a check, Dad. The second time you lied was tonight when you said that you had never told me a lie. That itself was a lie."

Dad wrote a check.

Perpetual

This really happened to me and our son.
It jogged a good memory for Barbara.

You've no doubt heard of perpetual motion of a mechanical device but have you ever heard of perpetual motion of a thought? This phenomenon was discovered by a seven-year-old boy in Minnesota when on a round-trip walk with his father. On this particular day they had invented a game to play along the way called "Most Unusual Things." Its objective was to observe objects or situations that could be considered new and unique. For example, on the first half of the walk they spotted a car with a Minnesota license plate in front and a Wisconsin plate on back. They also saw a uniquely carved house door and a building adorned with Christmas lights three months early.

Before departing they decided to make the game even more interesting with a contest that involved the two of them guessing how many unusual things they would actually find. The father guessed six and the boy guessed seven. The boy especially enjoyed this because his father had never beat him in one of their home-made contests.

Anyway, it was an entertaining walk. When they had nearly reached home the number of most unusual things was five. Suddenly the father noticed a three-legged squirrel and exclaimed, "Number six! Looks like I'm going to win!" Just before they reached the door the boy, who had lapsed deep into thought, stopped and smiling triumphantly stated, "No, Dad, I win."

"What? I guessed six and that's what we have."

"Yes, Dad," explained the boy, "but if we have six and you win then your winning a contest is a "most unusual thing" itself and that makes seven and I win.

Pausing a moment the father retorted, "But if we have seven then I haven't won and that's not unusual and so we drop back to six and I win."

And it continued: "Six, most unusual, makes seven and I win," "Seven, not unusual, back to six and I win." "Six, most unusual, makes seven and I win." This can go back and forth forever.

Perhaps the most unusual thing on that walk is the one not counted; that they had discovered a perpetual thought.

Vanity

Barbara didn't dislike vain people.
She was amused by them.

"World's Largest Viper" emblazoned a big sign above a glass cage in the new zoo. "That's my grandpa," the young snake proudly told his friends.

"Don't you dare admire that old geezer," scolded his mother. "He's nothing but a vain old fool. He could have been free like us, but no, he had to become a spectacle. He's so big because he's over-blown with pride." But the little snake was not convinced and he could envision himself one day being in the prestigious position of his grandpa. That very day he decided to spend every spare moment eating until he too would have his own cage and big sign.

The pond was the best place for food, especially at this time of year when it was filled with frogs. He sprang upon a large old bull, grabbing and securing a leg. The huge frog immediately bellowed, "Stop, stop, you don't want to eat me!"

"Yes, I do," replied the snake through the side of his mouth, "I want to eat you and all your family and friends until I become the world's biggest snake and have a cage in the zoo."

"But that will take years," responded the bull, "and I can get you in that new zoo within the week." The little reptile listened with interest as his prey continued. "I am what's called a 'genie frog' and I can grant you a wish."

"Great," said the snake. "Make me bigger than grandpa and I'll let you go." The frog explained that this wish had been used up by his grandpa who caught him by the leg the year before. But he had a better idea.

"I can give you legs, so many legs that you will become the fastest snake in the world. Just picture yourself in a cage next to your grandpa. Yes, I can see it now, the Worlds Fastest Viper next to the Worlds Largest Viper!"

No more convincing was needed. In a magic word and a "puff" the young snake had a hundred legs. He released the big frog and raced, really raced, to the zoo where he was readily accepted and given his own cage. But unfortunately for him it wasn't outdoors next to his grandpa. It was in a rather dark indoor room. He spent most of his time curled, in embarrassment, beneath the sign that boldly proclaimed "World's Largest Centipede."

Logic

Barbara loved to talk philosophy,
even when I made distortions of it.

The old physics professor stopped to rest on a campus park bench where a stranger was sitting. They exchanged niceties and the professor asked if the gentleman was with the college. "No," he said, pointing to the night sky. "I'm from a small planet of a star that is barely visible." He seemed harmless so the professor decided to humor him, asking how this was possible since physics says that distance is limited by the speed of light, and that we cannot time travel. "Your physics is correct," was the response, "and you cannot do these things, but our physics is also correct and we do them quite easily." The professor asked him to explain a little about his physics, to which the stranger replied, "I can't really do that. You wouldn't understand." The professor proudly related his credentials and assured him that he was very capable of understanding any type of science.

"Let me try to explain," said the stranger. "Science is simply the evolution of logic and your logic is on the wrong path to understanding such things. It's kind of like the tree charts you make depicting the evolution of species. There is a main trunk with many branches. The evolution of your gibbon, chimpanzee, and Neanderthal are on branches that have strayed off to a dead end. Only homo sapiens have followed the correct path to make it to the top of the tree. The evolution of logic has the same type branches and you believe that your logic is at the top. This is incorrect. Yours is on a side branch. You would have to back up considerably and take the correct path to understand higher logic and its subsequent science; probably an impossible task except for maybe a very young child. You may tell the child that two plus two is four and I may tell him it is five. We are both correct in our own logic. The path he takes in understanding the rationale behind either statement will determine his scientific potential."

"Well, at least he's done some thinking," thought the professor who was becoming increasingly amused. Patronizingly he asked if the stranger might at least offer a small hint to the nature of this expanded logic.

"Certainly," he replied after a moment of thought. "Quickly, think of the planet Earth. Stop. Think of the sun. Your thoughts have just traveled faster than the speed of light. And as for time travel, your memory frequently travels the past and your imagination the future."

"So much for nonsense," thought the professor and bid his farewell.

Embellishment

I prayed so hard that Barbara and I could grow old
together. I think I'd be just like this old guy
and Barbara would love it.

Johnny Carlson's parents had a special reason for visiting his grandpa. The old man had been at it again, embellishing stories with either nonsense or downright lies depending on the point of view. Johnny's parents had admonished him about this when Johnny was younger and Grandpa had modified children's stories such as telling him that Santa Claus wasn't jolly but cold and bellowed "I'm fr . . . fr . . fr . . . eezing and I want to go HO . . . HO . . . Ho . . . Home." Now they found that grandpa hadn't stopped. Johnny related fabulous tales such as the one about the leaning tower of Pisa that was really straight and the whole town of Pisa was leaning, and that dinosaurs were really small but had bones that swelled enormously in size when dead and exposed to air. After a stern reprimand, the old man agreed to stick to facts.

That afternoon when Johnny walked to Grandpa's house he was disappointed when the old man related the new rules. "But I really enjoy your stories, Grandpa," he said, "and I know when you're not telling the truth."

"I thought you knew," laughed Grandpa, "but if you want to hear any more you must not tell your parents." Johnny agreed and Grandpa started a wild story about the founding of America.

At the dinner table that evening his parents asked Johnny if Grandpa had told him a story. The young boy shrugged. "Johnny

Carlson, I asked you a question and I want an answer," demanded his mother. Sheepishly the little boy related that his grandpa had told him about who really discovered America.

"And," interrupted his father, "just who did he say discovered our country?"

"Christopher Columbus," he replied. His father looked at his mother and they sighed in relief.

Johnny, who had just finished his dinner walked away and in a very soft voice said to himself, "Christopher Columbus Carlson."

Luck

*We had been talking about our only trip to Las Vegas
the year before. We, eh, . . . broke even.*

The Lennox Avenue Irish Choir Club neither represented
Lennox Avenue nor a choir. It was a loosely woven group of
Irish Americans that was started in the 1960s by the Kelly brothers
and friends primarily as a ruse to get out of the house and away
from the family one night a week. At first they met at a small bar
on Lennox Avenue, thus the name. But as membership grew, they
rented space in a building several miles away and began collecting
dues and donating them to the choir of a local church because it
seemed to add an air of respectability to what was still pretty much
a "boys night out." Becoming a member of the LAICC required
little more than a signature, but young Will viewed his admit-
tance with pride. He was the youngest of the lot and in his first
year felt particularly privileged to be invited to their third annual
Las Vegas junket. The trip was a three-day event that entailed lots
of gambling and drinking and almost no sleep.

Waiting for a delayed flight home, Will took the opportunity
to ask his weary and red-eyed cohorts how they had fared at the
tables. To his surprise and delight his tallies showed that of the
thirty chaps no one had actually lost money. Ten had won and the
rest broke even. That night he began to think that all the bragging about the "luck of the Irish" might be more than fantasy.
Perhaps, he thought, it was true. After all, his group was all Irish
and nobody had lost.

In the following weeks, Will became so obsessed with this notion that he decided to withdraw a sizeable portion of his savings and make a solo trip back to Las Vegas. Waiting for departure he ran into an old schoolmate, an affable and bright fellow but who could never belong to the LAICC because he was so obviously English. After chatting a while, Will related his plan, to which his friend listened attentively, especially upon hearing that all of the club's members had either won or broke even. Finding a pause amongst the enthusiastic rambling he asked, "And how did you do yourself, Will?"

After an uncharacteristic hesitation, Will replied, "Me? Oh well, I, eh, I pretty much broke even." His voice regained spirit. "Yes, indeed, maybe even a bit ahead."

After his friend's parting, Will's smile dropped. He sat deep in somber thought for many minutes before getting up and heading home.

The Oak

Often we'd spend quiet time watching
a big tree outside the window.

You just couldn't tell when Kenny was serious or joking so the rest of the philosophy students at the outing were skeptical when he returned to the group with a somber face, claiming that that he had just had a conversation with an oak tree. He said that he had leaned against the tree for some time and upon leaving looked up at its stately depths and said in jest, "I must be going now, my friend; not all of us can just stand here doing nothing the rest of our lives." Then, as his story went, a deep voice from within the big oak bellowed a long somber oration that Kenny paraphrased as "Nothing! Nothing! I will be the home and shelter for scores of living creatures. How many do you plan to shelter and help? I will give man and beast life-sustaining oxygen and provide food and nourishment, enabling the earth to create thousands of new lives. How many will you feed and nourish? I will provide great joy, the playground for children and animals, the inspiration for song and poem, and the haunt for lovers and thinkers like yourself. What are your plans for providing happiness? I will be strong and constant and be viewed by both artist and layman with awe. How many people will you awe? And what's more I will live all my life creating only good and no harm or disappointment, and never ask for anything in return. How many will you harm in your future? How many will you disappoint? How many demands will you put upon your fellow man? Come back in thirty years and we shall compare our lives."

You just couldn't tell when Kenny was serious or joking.

Froghorn

To this one Barbara remarked,
"This isn't one of your homemade jokes is it?"

Before the invention of the warning horn, foggy weather was always a danger to ships, especially near port. Collisions with docks and other craft were a commonplace occurrence. This all changed when a brilliant military commander in ancient Athens came up with an idea. He tied a couple of frogs to the head of spears that lined the harbor docks. When boats approached, even in dense fog, the alert amphibians began to croak, serving warning that dockage was near. Harbor collisions were all but eliminated and the devices became widely known as "Frog Horns."

Widely known, that is, except to the Spartans who were bitter enemies of the Athenians and had little access to their navigational grapevine. One night they attempted a surprise attack on an Athenian port, relying on a thick fog to hide their presence. Approaching slowly they began to hear the croaking of frogs but dispelled it as merely the mating season. Unfortunately for them, a harbor guard also heard the croaks and awoke the commander who rapidly deployed his men to the docks. The men arrived just as the Spartans were landing and, grabbing the frog laden-spears, went on the offensive. The battle lasted only an hour, and ended with a Greek victory.

When the fog lifted, the commander found the chief of the Spartan fleet lying on a dock, badly wounded with a spear protruding from his neck. "Did you really think you could attack us and win?" asked the commander of his barely conscious foe. The fallen leader did not reply but one of his cohorts did with the now famous line, "He can't talk. He's got a frog in his throat."

Without

*Barbara and I had been talking
about our school days and teachers.*

It may have been one of the last one-room schoolhouses, but the township was small and had only twenty children of elementary age. The school's size, however, was compensated for by what the community felt was an excellent teacher who genuinely inspired her little students toward academic and compassionate studies. And the kids loved her, especially her experiments that involved the whole class. Probably the one they liked best occurred the year before when each Thursday afternoon they played a game that she called "without" that was designed to show them empathy for less fortunate children.

On the first Thursday she explained the experiment and told them that they would get a chance to see how it feels to be "without" eyes. Each child covered his eyes with a blindfold and they spent the entire afternoon without sight, improvising their studies to compensate for the handicap. At the end of the day the kids felt that in a small way they did understand how difficult it must be for children who are blind.

In subsequent weeks she had the kids pick the "without" subject and for the next many weeks the class went from physical impairments like being "without" arms to mental ones like being "without" senses of humor. With the former they tied their arms to their sides for the afternoon and with the latter they were not allowed to laugh or even smile.

After many weeks the children could hardly wait for Thursday afternoons, coming to class brimming with new "without" ideas. Then on one particular Thursday afternoon, little Billy's mother noticed him at home playing in the back yard. She was aghast. Had he played hooky or even worse been kicked out of school? She ran to him and demanded an explanation. "Everything's okay, Mom," he said. "I'm out of school today because it was my turn to pick the "without." His "without" was to be without a school.

Politics

There was just something about frogs that we both liked.

Talk about dirty tricks in politics! During the heated presidential election of 1944, the Democrats were quite worried about losing the rural vote. In a desperate measure their national campaign manager came up with a most devious ploy. He hired thousands of college students all over the country to teach frogs, who are actually very fast studies, to say the name "Roosevelt." In just a few months a large proportion of the nation's frogs could be heard croaking "Roosevelt . . . Roosevelt . . . Roosevelt." Because of this publicity tact Roosevelt easily won the election over Dewey and frog training ended.

Without refresher courses of any kind, the frogs soon began to lose retention of the entire name and in only a few years their utterings deteriorated from "Roosevelt" to "Roovelt" to "Rovet" and finally to "Rvet," the sound we hear today.

Of some interest is that when Dewey campaigners got wind of the Roosevelt scheme they tried a similar gimmick. It was, of course too late to have much effect on the election, but one can still hear its remnants today. Have you ever awakened early on a bright morning and heard a small bird atop a distant tree piping, "Dueee . . . Dueee . . . Dueee"?

Eggs

And back to the old reliable favorite: amphibians.

Although frogs and turtles are usually the best of friends, they do not get along very well in restaurants. Some say it's because the turtle is jealous that the frog can jump to his chair so fast, while others claim that the frog gets annoyed with the crunching sound the turtle makes when eating hard shell tacos.

But the truth is that this animosity started about six hundred years ago when the leader of the frog community was having a friendly lunch with his counterpart of the turtle community. Somehow they decided not only to order a delicacy, snake eggs, but to have a contest to see who could eat the most, with the winner paying the bill. After an hour the frog was gorged and could eat no more. The turtle continued for another half hour consuming a huge number of eggs and easily winning the wager. Even though the bill was expensive the frog paid in a sportsman-like manner.

This surely wasn't an incident worthy of causing centuries of bitterness between frogs and turtles at restaurants. What did bring it to this magnitude was when the frog later found that the turtle wasn't eating the expensive eggs at all. He was stuffing them in a little known hollow compartment between his body and shell. The final insult came when shortly after lunch the frog saw the turtle selling the eggs to members of the frog community for a dime a piece.

Salmon

I fished a lot, Barbara a little, but she caught
the biggest walleye and she never let me forget it.

A fine looking salmon in the prime of life awoke one morning to find his friends preparing for a trip. "Where we goin'?" he asked.

"We're going home," replied his best friend Ralph.

"Home?" he said, "I don't remember a home."

"Neither do I," continued Ralph, "but I know it's a stream a long way from here."

"Great!" enthused the salmon. "I love streams, basking in the shallow water, jumping for flies and mosquitoes."

"Oh no," quipped his friend solemnly, "this will be all work, swimming against strong currents and wracking our bodies over jagged rocks while desperately leaping rapids and falls."

"Well, I suppose, if that's what it takes to get home," he said after a moment's thought. "Count me in."

"Then," continued Ralph, "we reach the calm waters of home where our bodies become so feeble and distorted that we die."

"What! Are you out of your mind? We go home to die? Are you kidding? That's sheer lunacy. Why would anyone be so crazy?"

"To spawn," Ralph replied. "We go home to spawn and then we die."

"Look, Ralph. I'm healthy and normal and enjoy a good spawn as much as any other fish but I sure as heck ain't gonna die for it."

"Have it your own way," replied his serious friend while swimming off with a host of other salmon.

All the way to the stream, he tried to talk sense to his friends but they were intent on this voyage of doom. He kept thinking that they had all either gone nuts or that this was one unbelievable spawn.

Arguing all the way he swam halfway up the stream with his friends and then stopped and yelled, "No way! No way! I'm not going to die for a spawn! Not me! That's not the way I'm gonna die!"

And he was correct. Moments later he was scooped up by a bear and devoured.

Lorelei

*Barbara asked that I eventually send these stories
to our only grandchild, Lorelei, for future reading.
"She'll like this one " Barbara said.*

L orelei was a beautiful enchantress who sat on a big rock at the shore of the river Rhine. Every day boaters would pass and become awestruck by her angelic appearance. Steering their boats to shallower water to get a closer look at this charming siren, they would inevitably crash into the rocks and perish. This went on for years until one day a boat with only one man aboard approached. To her amazement this boatman smiled and waved but held his sturdy craft on course. "What?" she thought. "Am I losing it? Is my beauty fading?" In a tearful sprint she ran home to scrutinize herself in a mirror. Finding no changes she gradually felt better.

The next day Lorelei took extra care in preparing her face and wore her most seductive dress. A record five boats crashed into the rocks that day but her lone boatman didn't appear. She wore the same outfit for two more days when finally, to her delight, she saw him in the distance. Posing her most enticing stance and smiling her most beguiling smile she watched in amazement as he passed by, again with only a smile and a wave. She was infuriated that he didn't stop. What's worse, he was handsome, very handsome. Who could this man be? He had to be very intelligent, not risking his boat on the rocks, and he was probably very wise, not being lured by her charms. She pouted all night until a thought arose. Maybe this man had poor eyesight. That's it! That's surely it! She was relieved.

Three days later he again appeared, waving and smiling, the sunlight glistening off his glasses. "Glasses?!" she exclaimed. "He has to be able to see me!" That was it. Her curiosity had run the gamut. She had to know more about this most handsome, intelligent, and wisest of men. Sitting on her rock continually for two more days, she waited anxiously. Finally he appeared. Lorelei sprang to her tiny wooden boat and rowed to the center of the river. He drew nearer and nearer until she could at last see him clearly. She stood up and, with genuine enthusiasm, cried out, "Grandpa John!"

Shortages

*Cheese and frogs: Perfect ingredients
for a story for Barbara.*

During the great cheese shortage of 1630 it was difficult to find even a small piece of this suddenly valuable commodity. Even a little morsel to place on a mousetrap was very expensive and mouse trappers were hard pressed to find a substitute. Eventually they captured flies, who were weak from a cheeseless diet and easy to catch, and tried placing them on the platforms of their traps. To their astonishment they caught no mice, but often the trap was sprung and a sticky coiled blob of gooey material was resting on the platform. They were perplexed, having no idea that these were actually the severed tongues of frogs who had attempted to remove the flies. Because of this strange phenomenon they nearly abandoned using flies as bait. But then an especially creative trapper realized that these sticky blobs were ideal for hanging pictures and also for attaching false mustaches. Soon they became the rage of the village and tongue trapping became very popular.

Eventually most of the frog community was tongueless and desperate to find an alternative food to the flies they could no longer catch. Their choice turned out to be earthworms, not only because they were easy to catch but because medical books said they were excellent for the regrowth of tongues. This was great for the frogs, but soon began to have a devastating effect on the villagers who earned their income from catching fish and suddenly had difficulty finding their bait of choice, earthworms.

By this time the cheese shortage had ended and, wouldn't you know it, they discovered that fish love cheese. As their catches improved they began to use more and more of this wonderful new bait until, you guessed it, there was another shortage of cheese. Once again cheese was banned as mousetrap bait, flies became weak, and a whole new generation of tongued frogs had arrived. The cycle repeated itself and it has continued to do so every five years to this very day.

Brevity

Barbara enjoyed an earlier story about
a potential romance. So another.

"Wow!" he said to himself. "Who is that heavenly creature?" The library was rather busy that day but she stood out like a brilliantly shining angel. To his instantly fascinated eyes it actually seemed that she was shrouded by some type of mystical celestial vapor. "Am I dreaming?" he thought. "Is she real?" Almost involuntarily he rose from his seat and approached her. He stood transfixed, in a stupor of awe as her slender arm floated gently upward toward a book on the top shelf. In an awkward gesture to get her attention he blurted, "Uh, sorry to bother you. I'm . . . uh . . . uh . . . John. Can I help you reach that book?" She slowly lowered her arm and with a smile that nearly knocked him from his feet replied, "Very well." Completely transfixed he handed her the book and stumbled dumbfounded back to his chair. Regaining his senses he mused at her single words "very well."

"How gentle, how ethereal these two softly spoken words," he thought. "Very well, very well," he mused repeatedly to himself.

It was many minutes before he collected himself sufficiently to approach her a second time and, again, he was awkward, stunned by her delicately clad white satin figure and long flowing golden hair. "I see you're looking at Checkov stories," he stammered. "Old Anton was quite a writer."

Her smile sent a shivers down his spine as she replied, "Indeed."

Once again he was spellbound and could only wander back to his chair. "Indeed," he mumbled. "That's all she said. Indeed. Indeed. How quaint, how charming, how beautiful."

He fared no better at his third and fourth attempts to strike up a conversation, but did carry back to his chair two more single words: "perhaps," and "quite." For some unknown reason these short and tender replies made her even more exciting and mysterious. Convinced she was the heavenly goddess he had always dreamed of, he was determined not to let her slip away. Gathering his wits he made a final approach and in a quickly practiced and now steady voice asked, "Would you like to have coffee?"

She turned to him and he could instantly tell by her warm smile that she would consent, and probably in a single dainty word. Her lips parted and in a soft angelic voice she replied, "Get lost, asshole."

Country Club

Barbara never pressured me to make money.
She would have accepted any economic lifestyle but
I think it was her love that guided me to do all right.

Money can buy many things but not a membership into the White Hills Country Club. Oh, you have to be wealthy but you must also be selected by its chairman to fill one of the rarely vacated seats. This year there is such a vacancy and Harold Browne, one of the few candidates for the prestigious position, sits at the club's bar. He has just completed his final interview with the chairman and laments to the bartender that he will probably not be seeing him again. A little prodding and the bar-keep finds that the candidate fears that the source of his wealth will not meet the high standards of the club. "Oh, I could have lied and said that I come from old money or that I worked my way up to the top of the industrial ladder," related Browne. "But I decided to tell it like it was and take my chances. You see, I made it to the top simply out of resentment and a stroke of luck."

He tells the story of how he was a lowly chemist for a marine supply company. One day he was told by the president that a chemist was no longer needed. Browne developed a bitter sense of resentment for this boss who he'd never liked. Two months later he received a condescending call from the president asking for a one-time project. It seems that a customer and yacht owner was looking for a solution to dock ropes scratching the hull of his new vessel. The president wanted Browne to develop a coating or some type of paint for the rope that would eliminate this abrasion. Browne said he'd try, all the time knowing a formula for just such a coating that he had made at home for his wife's clothes line. Two weeks later he called the president and told him that he had formulated a coating but that it was very expensive, $100 a gallon. He had actually bought the ingredients for $4 a gallon. Price was no object and the president ordered ten gallons. A sense of revenge was complete.

But Browne's story was not complete. The coating worked so well that other members of the yacht club where it had been used soon deluged the company with orders. Browne made an exclusivity contract with the company and began making the stuff for a living. Word of mouth spread and he began amassing huge profits that after five years made him wealthy. "You see, it was mostly luck," he concludes.

Browne does get appointed to White Hills. It seems the club's chairman had a somewhat similar rise to wealth. His was a bit simpler, however. In 1966 he was a lab tech and won the lottery.

Pirate

Groan, groan, groan, but she like it.

The pirate ran frantically from the police, his right-hand hook swinging in the air and his peg leg clicking on the cobblestone pavement. Just as he was making some headway he came to a busy intersection in the center of which was a manhole whose cover featured a square vent hole in its center. As the pirate scurried through the weaving traffic his peg leg landed directly in that hole and he was stopped in his tracks. Now I suppose you think I'm going to say something corny like "You can't put a round peg in a square hole," but I'm not because this is a serious story. Also, you can forcefully wedge a round peg into a square hole if the peg is tapered.

Anyway, there the pirate stood in the middle of the intersection waving his hand and hook frantically. The police were about to approach him and make their arrest when they noticed something most unusual. The pirate's waving extremities were actually directing traffic and in a most effective manner. The normally chaotic intersection now resembled at least some state of order and the police decided to leave well enough alone until the end of rush hour. They dropped into a beer hall and toasted their soon-to-be captive but upon returning to the street noticed that the only thing left on the manhole was the pirate's peg leg. He had unscrewed himself and escaped. No, I'm not going to say that he was captured and sued the police department but that the judge said he didn't have a "leg to stand on." I told you, this is a serious story.

What did happen was that the police immediately surrounded a nearby PegLeg-Mart, feeling it was his most likely destination. But they were wrong. He was in the Broom-Mart next door and had replaced his peg with a short broom and was now preparing to make a hasty getaway through the still busy streets. No, no, no, the headlines the next day didn't read "Pirate sweeps through downtown streets." Serious, remember, serious!

The pirate had gone just a few blocks when he heard police whistles and ducked into the Exotic Animal-Mart. He emerged moments later with a six-foot section of leash line tied to his hook on one end and the front legs of a skunk on the other. Waving his hook, the attached line, and its spray-emitting animal in swooping circles, the crowd dispersed rapidly, making a wide path for his last attempt at freedom. I say last attempt because moments later his broom got stuck in some fresh street tar, the skunk ran out of scent, and being rendered completely helpless, he was caught "hook, line, and stinker."

Elcalibara

Barbara loved horseback riding but didn't get a chance very often. She planned to correct this in the future.

Sir Reginald, frail and wrinkled with age, rests quietly in his favorite plush chair at London's oldest and most prestigious equestrian club. He is quite a contrast to the robust bronze cavalryman who sits upon the stately bronze steed in the courtyard. The magnificent statue, cast almost sixty years before, depicts Sir Reginald, the great national hero and the sole survivor of the famous Charge of the Last Brigade in which three hundred Englishmen rode bravely into the jaws of death, namely five thousand Arabian soldiers. For years this proud and famous horseman has repeated the story to countless groups of spellbound countrymen. Like the soliloquy of a seasoned actor his narration is fine-tuned in verbiage and intonation, soft and eerie when he and his comrades mount their splendid steeds in regal formation, and intense and powerful when the swords are drawn, the bugle sounds, and they speed into the path of their enemy at the far end of the valley. Sir Reginald, atop his gallant horse, Elcalibara, is at the head of the charge and with a mighty and selfless courage has smitten thirty Arabs before the rest retreated into the hills. Countless poems and inspired drawings have immortalized the scene of the retreat, the battlefield strewn with the fallen men and horses, and an exhausted but still sword-wielding Sir Reginald and his trusty Elcalibara, the only two survivors of the battle.

The now ninety-year-old hero had told the story so often that what really happened seemed like a fuzzy dream. He does remember his brave intent, his raising his sword and spurring Elcalibara to the charge. But Elcalibara did not move. Two hundred and ninety-nine galloping cavalry sped by as he sat anchored to that spot, kicking and verbally trying to urge his obstinate steed to action, but to no avail. Half an hour later the distant dust settled and he saw the retreating Arabs and the battlefield strewn with the dead. Elcalibara finally turned and they slowly retreated in the opposite direction. Despondent and bitter, Sir Reginald rode to the village where he had bought Elcalibara and demanded an explanation for this horse who had been so highly praised by its owner but proved a coward in combat.

It was a long ride back to the British outpost and he had a lot of time to think about his account of the battle. He molded this account carefully and decided to share the glory with his mount since she had certainly saved his life. He hadn't thought of her inaction in this way until her previous owner related that in Arabic Elcalibara means "very smart horse."

Zucchini

Part of this story is true. When we moved into our first house a neighbor gave us some zucchini that I unloaded at work.

Had his mother been there he'd have admonished her for neglecting to teach him one of the cardinal laws of a happy life: "Beware of free zucchini." But ignorant of this tenet he had naively accepted five of the huge, shiny green vegetables from a new neighbor. His wife, who like everyone else, had been taught about zucchinis at an early age was aghast. The problem, she explained, is that as a food zucchinis have few and questionable applications yet they just seem too valuable to throw away. Thus, owners of these bulbous garden misfits are constantly and desperately trying to unload them on ignorant acquaintances. He felt ridiculous, not only in accepting them but in thanking his neighbor profusely.

The next morning he lugged a big zucchini-laden box to his office, feeling certain that he could pawn off at least a couple of the five on fellow workers who were as witless as he had been. The thirty rejections were all short and to the point, "No," "No way," "Are you kidding?" etc.

But it did brighten the morning for his best friend and co-worker who delighted in his quandary. Laughing boisterously his friend told him, "I'll bet you five bucks a piece that you can't give those away by the end of the day."

Only his pride made him accept the bet.

"You owe me twenty-five bucks," he announced when his friend returned from lunch. "I unloaded the whole works to people on the second floor. In fact your wife took two of them." His friend protested in disbelief, especially since his wife who was noted in the company for her intellect would be far too bright to fall for any ruse involving zucchini. "But it's true," he insisted, "I just delivered them a few minutes ago."

"Aha," retorted his friend, "it can't be true! This is the day of the second floor's appreciation lunch and no one has returned yet. I just checked."

"I know," he calmly replied. "I called them before lunch and said I'd leave them on their desks." His friend quickly snapped his cell phone from its clip and dialed his wife who indeed was still at the restaurant.

"You didn't agree to take some vegetables from Harry, did you?" he barked.

"Vegetables?" was her response. "I thought watermelons were a fruit."

Best Gift

A little girl and her grandpa. Always works.

"Do you think Grandpa liked my gift? Are you sure?" These were her automatic questions on the way home from Christmas or his birthday or most any other holiday. It was heartening that a little seven-year-old girl should have such compassion for an old man. But he had always been her favorite. She loved his wit, his childish charm, and his penchant for funny anecdotes. The two had been close friends for as long as she could remember. She only worried that living by himself he might become bored or run out of the amusing little stories he saw in everyday life and loved to relate.

But this time she didn't ask. Her mother and father were puzzled. His birthday party had gone well, except perhaps for the "incident." Could it have been the "incident"? Was she upset? Did Grandpa embarrass her?

Grandpa had decided to cook dinner for the small family. Before its preparation he told his little grandchild that he would make her favorite meal. "What kind of meat do you like?" he asked. "Do you like fish?"

"Ugh," she replied, "I hate fish! The only kind of meat I really like is chicken." Then he found that she also loved lettuce but hated spinach. After an hour of secret preparation Grandpa presented them with a fine meal that he called "chicken and lettuce." The little girl gobbled it down as her parents watched in amazement. When she ran to the kitchen for a second helping they laughed, especially Grandpa. "Did you like my meal?" he asked when she returned. With a similar grin she nodded heartily, her little mouth full. "That makes me very happy," he said. "I guess I'm a real chef. I can hardly wait to tell friends."

"You didn't ask if Grandpa liked his gifts," her mother finally asked. "Is everything all right?"

"Oh yes," she replied. "I know he liked my best gift. The one where I ate his fish and spinach. I bet he'll have hours of fun telling that one to his friends!"

Uncle Ralph

Barbara expects me to swat back
when she boasts about her big walleye.

Daniel lies on the dock as his father and brother speed off across the lake. Next year, his dad told him, he would be old enough to join them on their early morning expedition. It was okay for him to fish with them during the day but the early morning was reserved for the older, more avid fishermen. But Daniel always woke up early to see them off, hoping that Dad would change his mind. Almost asleep he peered through the last crack in the dock when suddenly his eyes bulged and his heart stopped. A huge walleye slid silently through the water below him and spying him stopped and seemed to flap its tail fin as if to say "hello." Daniel was stunned as the two stared at each other. Then he remembered his can of worms within arms reach. Without losing eye contact he quietly grasped the can and felt his way to its contents that revealed a large night crawler. Slowly he dropped the slimy morsel through the crack. The huge walleye waited for a second and then gobbled it down and eased off to deeper water.

This turned out to be the beginning of a long friendship. Each morning the small boy returned to the dock with a treat and each morning his new fish friend slid into view and grabbed its welcome breakfast, vacuuming it into its gaping mouth and then nodding as if to say "thanks" before moving on. Daniel named his friend Morgan after his grandfather. Daniel kept Morgan a secret throughout the summer and often felt that his ritual encounter was even better than fishing with his dad and brother.

Then one morning horror struck. A strong wind made it too risky to travel by boat. His dad headed back to the cabin but his brother decided to cast off the dock. Daniel stood aghast as his brother's pole suddenly bent violently and he let out with a "whoa" as he began to reel in an obviously large catch. Rushing back to the dock his father helped coach in a walleye of huge proportions. "Morgan!" the small boy shuttered in disbelief.

He was in shock as his brother and dad ran to the cabin to show off the trophy. In tears he dropped to the dock and peered through the crack into the empty water where he knew his friend would never again appear. Then the unbelievable happened. Just as had happened so many mornings before, Morgan did appear.

In ecstasy Daniel grabbed a giant earthworm from his can and dropped it through the crack. But Morgan did not devour his treat this time and he did not wave his tail in customary delight. Instead he looked up sadly at the boy and lamented, "How can I eat when I've just lost Uncle Ralph?"

Palindrome

Sometimes we talked about silly words. "Poop" was one.

A palindrome is a name or word or phrase or anything that is spelled the same backwards as forwards, such as Bob or Dad or poop. I will never forget this because "palindrome" caused me to lose an important contest when I was in high school. Years before when I was about ten, I hung around with the scrawny school "brain." One day the school bully, Bob, was teasing and shoving my friend. When he could take no more, my friend, who was usually clean spoken, reared back and yelled "You . . . you . . . you . . . Palindrome," as if the word was so terrible that it was hard to speak it. This incensed Bob, who chased and beat the tar out of my friend. Well, I had no idea of what a palindrome was but I knew it was something really bad. When I couldn't find it in the dictionary (probably because I thought it was polimdrone), I knew it was taboo.

I didn't hear the word again until one day when my Dad and I had one of our rare verbal fights. Losing the argument I finally screamed, "You polimdrone!" and ran from the room. I was surprised that he didn't chase after me and really give me heck. He was probably too shocked. (Now I know that he probably thought I meant "Dad.")

It was high school when I next came upon this nemesis of a word. I had become quite studious and had entered the school trivia contest, a big deal in those times. I was an odds-on favorite and was on stage with nine other finalists. My family and friends watched as they gave us the first, and supposedly easiest, question. It was "Name a palindrome found around the house." My god! I panicked. What could be as terrible or nasty as a "palindrome" and be found around the house? My labored answer got roars from all over the auditorium. It was "dog poop." Embarrassed as I have ever been I left the stage, not understanding what one of the judges meant when he whispered as I passed by, "If you'd said just "poop" alone we would have given you credit."

Wolf's Revenge

And back to animals and an imaginary world.

Long ago there lived three pigs who were good friends. The first pig built a house of straw. It took the second pig longer to build his house of wood. It took the third pig a very long time and a lot more money to build his house of brick. One day a big bad wolf approached the straw house and roared, "I'm going to huff and puff and blow your house down!" The pig ran out the back door just in time and scurried to the wooden house to warn his friend.

The wolf soon arrived at the wooden house but as he was bellowing his threat, the two pigs, who had hidden behind him, tied his tail to a tree with a rope. The wolf blew the house down and, running to catch the pig he thought was inside, came to a screeching and painful halt. The two pigs came out of hiding and, staying just out of his reach, laughed uncontrollably and taunted him with sarcastic verbiage, after which they threw rotten apples and poked him with a stick. The wolf, who from the start was just playing out an old fairy tale and meant no real harm, was furious and pledged revenge. But the pigs weren't worried because they would stay at their friend's brick house.

That afternoon the three pigs were taking a nap in the brick house when the wolf sneaked in the back door and quietly put his plan into action. Then he went back outside and yelled through the window in a monstrous roar, "Fire! Fire! Fire!" The pigs, in a state of panic, jumped up then fell down then got up again and stumbled back down, twisting and turning and bumping into one another. The wolf shook with laughter so intense that tears flew from his eyes. In a state of utter jubilation he walked off into the woods, his bandaged tail wagging like an excited puppy.

He could hardly wait to tell the family about his revenge and when his wife came home from work he sat her and the kids around the kitchen table and told them the whole story. At its conclusion his laughter was such that he could barely get the words out, especially the last part. "And I snuck into their house while they were sleeping and tied their shoelaces together."

Grandpa

*Barbara laughed and knew I was talking
about myself in old age.*

It seemed that every time she visited Grandpa had a new theory on people or human nature. He had spare time and spent much of it wandering about town observing people, especially enjoying retail shops and malls. He'd run experiments like leaving half a five-dollar bill sticking out from the pages of a phone book to observe the reaction of passersby or walking with eye patches and a white cane to see if he was given less or more attention. As usual he had a new theory this time and was excited to demonstrate. Proclaiming that he had discovered a method to evoke more respect from strangers, he placed into his shirt pocket a wooden tongue depressor that he had filched from his doctor's office the week before. Responding to her quizzical look he explained that the tongue depressor suggested to strangers that he was a doctor and thus he was treated with the respect given physicians. "This and an owlish facial expression is all it takes!" he enthusiastically claimed. "I've tried it! More people greet me, and they say 'hello' instead of 'hi' and talk to me with an air of esteem. It's great. We must go to the mall and I'll show you."

He was elderly so she obliged his whim. Soon they were at the bank in the shopping center. The plan was that he'd approach an especially grouchy-looking teller and cash a check. From nearby she'd subjectively evaluate the amount of respect he received. And, by gosh, his plan seemed to work. An extra portion of attention did seem to be paid him. Grandpa was exuberant on hearing her observations and insisted that she now cash a check so they could observe what would surely be an inferior response.

Taking her check the teller asked, "I saw you standing with that old man. Is he your grandfather?" She affirmed and he continued, "I don't know him but I often see him walking about the stores talking to strangers and taking notes. He must be quite an interesting man."

"Oh, yes," she responded. "He's becoming a bit senile and forgetful but he's definitely interesting."

"Not to be nosey," he added, "but speaking of forgetfulness, you might remind him to take that popsicle out of his shirt pocket before it melts."

Little Bro

She also laughed when I told imaginary tales of my youth.

She sat deep in thought, arms akimbo and long satin hair glistening in the bright schoolroom light. She was frustrated with her younger brother. She would simply tell him that this was the last time she would be the tester for one of his weird inventions. Being his only sibling and enamored by his enthusiasm to reinvent the world she had felt obliged to encourage him and test his ideas. But this time his invention made her half an hour late for school and it had to end.

His latest was a new type of hair brush. He had rationalized that cats have smooth silky hair and they don't use a comb or brush with bristles. They simply use their tongues. So his invention was a piece of slimy soft rubber attached to a handle. She tried it that morning and it took half an hour to make her hair presentable. This had to be the end!

Suddenly a slim angular classmate ambled by. "Nice hair!" he commented and smiled. My gosh! She'd had her eye on this guy for a long time and he'd never even noticed her before. Wow! She pondered for some time and then silently told herself, "Well, maybe I can wake up half an hour early every day.

Rendezvous

*After Barbara's death I occasionally made stories
to help create memories of our last months together.*

How many times she had sat in this long grass with her head resting against the wrinkled bark of the ancient oak. And now, twenty years later, nothing had changed, nothing except that she was alone. He would not keep the pact they had made so long ago to meet here on this very date. But that was all right. The pact was born from the romanticism of two idealistic young spirits. One must expect how easily the stoicism of time can erase teenage dreams. After all, she, who was twice married with children, had traveled the three hundred miles merely out of some strange girlish whim. He had probably forgotten altogether. So she was disappointed but not really upset, even after three hours had passed.

The serene calm actually sharpened her memories, which would not disappoint. She could almost see his slim muscular body splashing in the distant pond and later rushing back to her with dandelions he had picked on the run. His face was so clean and vibrant that it stirred her heart. She could hear his quiet voice reading from a book of poetry or crackling with enthusiasm when they discussed philosophy. And when he tried to sing, it was so funny. Why, she smiled to herself, was it so hard for him to be serious when they kissed? She guessed he was just too happy. Another hour passed and it was becoming dark.

"Your visit must have gone well. You sure were gone long enough," her sister remarked when she returned to the hotel.

"Oh," she replied, "it was great in a way but also sad. I have grown so old and he didn't seem to have changed at all."

Fortune

With Barbara gone, the subject didn't seem to matter but
it often centered around death and a lack of happiness.

The streets were narrow and cluttered with shops, but very few people were out walking on that drizzly afternoon. The three young sailors had made a wrong turn while looking for nightclubs and somehow found themselves lost in this dingy part of Singapore. They were anxious and stepped into a dark and gloomy little boutique to ask directions. Inside sat an ancient Chinese woman wearing a pitch-black dress and a spidery veil. Upon inquiry, there was a long pause and she replied in a low eerie voice, "I'll read your fortune, then I'll give you directions." Realizing that her business was that of soothsaying and that she was probably a fraud, they balked.

"And how much will this bilking cost us, old witch?" asked the first sailor sarcastically. Her face became wrought with a countenance of fear as she peered into the eyes of each of them almost simultaneously.

"It will be brief and cost you nothing," was her ominous reply. The aura of the tiny shop suddenly became placid and the sailors no longer smiled.

"Oh, what the hell, get it over with then," said the first. She asked them to stand together and gaze into her eyes. Moments passed and she gave them an omen.

Pointing a decrepit bony finger at the sailors she proclaimed, "You will each be very happy only one more time."

The three were quiet for some time and then suddenly, as if breaking from a trance, burst into laughter. The second man pulled a dollar from his pocket and threw it on her lap.

"Here you are, old lady, keep it." He winked. "We'll find our own way out of this hellhole." And they did find their way to the lively section of town and drank and danced and had a grand time until nearly dawn. Staggering back to port the first sailor shouted, "I really needed that after three months at sea. I haven't been so happy in a long time!" Just as his sentence ended, a truck veered out of nowhere and struck him dead.

The next weeks were filled with grief for the remaining two sailors. Once one of them brought up the old lady's omen but they promptly dismissed it as a coincidence. A few days, later when the second sailor received a letter from his girlfriend accepting his recent proposal of marriage, he jumped up and down with jubilation and yelled, "I've never been so happy!" Then he dropped to the floor dead. The official cause was a stroke, unusual at his age but not unprecedented.

But the third sailor knew instantly that the odds were way too small and that the culprit had to be the omen. He vowed that he would not put himself in a position to be happy, at least until he could get back to Singapore and talk to the old lady. But a couple of months later, when he returned, her shop seemed to have disappeared.

The next forty-five years were sheer misery for this last sailor. He never partied, never drank, never married, and avoided any type of praise or commendation for fear of becoming very happy. He lived by himself, worked at a menial job, rarely talked to people, and never read or viewed anything humorous. In fact he managed not to even laugh once since his two mates died so many years ago.

Finally, in his seventies, he had a heart attack and lay in the hospital on what the doctors were certain was his deathbed. He was given the prognosis and closed his eyes awaiting the end. "But wait!" he suddenly thought. "I've been worried about dying all my life because of that damn curse. What have I been worrying about? That old bitch said I'd have one more time of real happiness. I can't die until then. I could live forever. That wasn't a bad omen, it was a good one." He opened his eyes and shouted in revelation "I will be immortal." His heart filled with joy and for the first time in nearly a half century he became very happy.

Ending It All

Until modern times the most common form of suicide amongst frogs was either sitting in front of a hungry snake or lying down with legs raised by the back door of a fine restaurant. With the advent of skyscrapers, however, some depressed frogs began to mimic a form more commonly employed by humans. Many of these jumping-from-a-tall-building attempts failed when the leap of the frog was so great that he simply landed on top of an adjacent building.

The most famous such attempt occurred in 1956 in New York City when a bullfrog was fired from his job and decided to end it all by jumping from the observation deck of the Empire State Building. His leap was of such proportion that he actually landed on the wing of a Miami-bound jet liner that was flying overhead. The story did have a happy ending though. The plane was hijacked to Cuba where the frog earned a position on their Olympic long jump team. He won a silver medal the following year.

Mack Truck

Barbara used to tell me when I'd go for a walk,
"Be careful. Don't get hit by a Mack truck."

One little drunken mistake and it haunted him the rest of his life. It happened when Gilbert was on leave from the Navy in San Francisco. He and two buddies decided to check out a rumor about an amazing fortune-teller in the rundown wharf district of the city. In a small, shabby, ill-lit shop, they finally located Madam M who fascinated them with her powers of revealing all sorts of past secrets about the three. Then, as they were about to leave, one of them asked Madam M if she could predict how they would each die. The old lady was shocked at the request and denied it until they pulled out enough dollars to entice her to make a prediction against her better judgment. But it didn't seem shocking to them, rather more comical. The first was to die falling off an elephant. The second was to die from laughter, and Gilbert himself was to die by being run over by a Mack truck.

The incident was forgotten until ten years later when Gilbert decided to locate his friends to organize a reunion. To his horror he found that his first friend had stayed with the Navy and died on a shore leave in India when, on another drunken night, he fell off the huge statue of an elephant and broke his neck. His second friend had left the service and done very well in private life but died one night at a ceremony in his honor when a joke was told and he choked on a chicken bone while laughing uncontrollably.

Madam M's predictions came back to him clearly and he was aghast. It had to be more than a coincidence and from that day on he took elaborate efforts to stay off any road that might harbor a Mack truck. His efforts forced him to become almost a recluse, not even daring to venture out on the shortest of walks or drives. And it worked. He devoted his life to proving Madam M wrong and would often wake in the middle of the night after a dream in which he died of natural causes and in his last breath exclaimed, "You were wrong Madam M! You were wrong!" For forty years he successfully avoided any truck traffic and indeed was still alive.

Then one night, aged and ailing from heart problems and arthritis, he had more than his usual two nightcaps and in a moment of rebellion and bravado walked out onto the street in front of his little house for the first time in four decades. He looked in both directions and grinned. Suddenly and apparently out of nowhere a huge speeding truck appeared and came to a screeching halt after running him down. The driver backed up leaving the fatally struck old man peering up at the monstrous vehicle. But the driver had no idea what the crumpled figure meant when in his last breath he smiled and said, "You were wrong Madam M" and why his eyes did not close but remained transfixed on the huge hood ornament and letters that clearly spelled out "Kenworth."

Alph 1

I isolated myself up north and began creating
some imaginary friends. Alph supposedly
was named for alpha or a beginning.

The yolk was a challenge. He blended the yolks of several chicken eggs to make a slurry but must now somehow gel the yellow mass to make one large yolk. And preservatives must be added. The whole project would backfire if it rotted. But neither of these problems are insurmountable. Alph has spent many years experimenting with materials and chemicals and within the hour he has one fine large yolk that suspends itself nicely in the preserved albumen he'd prepared earlier. Now he has only to carefully place the mixture into an opening in the large eggshell that he'd crafted with great effort from crushed shells and plaster of Paris. Then after he mends the hole, which would take hours of patching and sanding, his masterpiece egg would be complete. Alph was happy with the size. It wasn't large, say the size of a basketball, but was big enough to stir one's imagination, easily larger than that of any living bird.

Early the next morning Alph would place his egg and its straw nest in a marshy area adjacent to a pond where local business people and college students often spent lunch lounging and wading and enjoying the scenery. He would tuck his project just out of sight but where he felt someone would find it. It was far from the residential lakes where he had placed artificial shark teeth the year before. In a spot of mud that he had also prepared that week he would make the slight footprint of an imaginary huge bird. Alph was especially proud of the wooden foot he used to make the impression. He loved carving, especially in pine.

And that was that. He would never see the egg again. You see, Alph had a rather strange streak. He loved to play this type of joke ever since he retired and became faced with a more meaningful solution to a lifetime of recurrent boredom. His only rules were that the project must challenge his creativity and that he would not see the outcome. The latter was especially important since it was imperative that he would get what he called "fodder" for his imagination: a host of possible outcomes that he could ponder and dream about during long and lonely winter nights.

Many folks would consider Alph not so much an artisan, for which his talent surely qualified him, but a nut.

Alph II

For some unexplained reason it was important that Alph rarely watched the outcome of his pranks. He probably felt that he could always conjure up an ending in his dreams that could not be matched by reality. But in the case of the giant egg, nest, and footprint he placed near the community lake, he was caught off guard. On the third page of the local newspaper his eye caught the heading of an article entitled "Unusual Egg Baffles College Professors." He didn't read the article but couldn't help but think of an oversight on his part. "I should have mixed a bit of human and animal saliva into the yolk to make any DNA sampling more interesting," he thought. But that was okay, he was off on a little vacation, a train trip to the West Coast and his mind would be off of tricks for a while. Well, that is except for the lottery prank that he always employed when traveling. He liked to play the scratch-off ticket version where he removed all the waxy coating from the losers and painted over the playing area with a silvery permanent enamel that was impossible to scratch away. He'd place these on public tables or benches or in telephone stalls. On occasion he would watch their finders struggle with fingernails, coins, or even pocket knives, all to no avail.

On the train Alph became acquainted with a natty older gentleman who was traveling on business. It was a three-day trip and during one of their visits his new friend suggested a game of cards. Alph was reluctant, not because he didn't like cards or wasn't talented at most games, but because of a cheating phobia. He found it too tempting. But resolved to honest play, he agreed to gin rummy, which the two played for many hours during the next two days. The cheating temptation turned out not to be a problem. You see, it took only one hand for Alph to discover that his partner was a cheater with no qualms and Alph enjoyed the cheating just enough to keep the games even.

His playing partner eventually became quite frustrated at his inability to beat Alph. They had started playing for a nickel a point but by the end of the second day his chagrined opponent had slowly increased the ante. But this made no difference in the outcome. However, knowing that he was marked as a dupe from the beginning, Alph was kindhearted and decided to alleviate the financial anticipation of his partner, who after all did have an engaging personality and made the long trip seem short. As a gesture of finality he suggested that they play one last game for a hundred dollars.

Alph was dealt a beautiful hand and it took all his talent to lose, but he did manage to do so and his friend was genuinely pleased for the first time in two days. Alph offered a personal check for his loss but explained that it shouldn't be cashed until he got home in a week and could make a deposit. "Unless," he said, "you'd be willing to accept well over a hundred lottery tickets that I've been collecting for my granddaughter." His partner accepted the tickets and they departed with a firm handshake.

"What the heck," thought Alph. "I guess one giant delight is worth a hundred small ones."

Alph's Granddaughter

Alph just had to have a granddaughter.

Lorie delighted in giving her grandpa verbal "wooden nickels." Her latest was in the form of a short letter in which she proposed that Alph change his name to something old-fashioned such as Melvin or Harold or Abraham. In a vein of utter seriousness she suggested that this would make him live longer. Her rationale was that in observing obituaries in the newspaper she noted that the people who lived long lives all had old-fashioned names.

And Alph delighted in respondinging to such silliness. He now calls her Matilda. He also enjoyed bouncing bits of philosophy off her bright young brain. Since retiring Alph had dwelled more and more on the meaning of life and had come to the conclusion that selfishness is the curse of mankind and that its opposite, charity, is the only true virtue. "Making people happy is the one true path to a rewarding life," he decided.

He was very serious about this and tried to make it his major goal. He lamented that he was not a musician or an artist. "A musician can play one piece of music and make hundreds of people happy," he mused. Perhaps his pranks and charity would suffice in making others happy. He wrote to Lorie and enclosed twenty dollars in the envelope. "I want you to make someone happy by giving them this money," he wrote, "and then let me know how you feel. Remember that it is better to give than to receive."

He was pleased to receive a reply so soon. "Your idea really works, Grandpa, even better that you probably thought. I gave the owner of the toy store the twenty dollars. This made him very happy. So happy, in fact, that he gave me twenty dollars worth of toys. This made me very happy. Your money made two people very happy."

Alph was amused at her witty reply but a bit disappointed that she did not grasp the true meaning of his gesture. When he talked to her next he hinted that she might have given the idea more thought. "But I did, Grandpa," she answered. "I understand that it is better to give than to receive but we can't all be givers because for every giver there must be a receiver. So the best we can hope for is half-givers and half-receivers."

"Hmm," thought Alph. "Maybe she's onto something. Maybe we are all more givers in our lives than we might think. The musician makes people happy with his music but so does the garbage collector by keeping things clean and the engineer by creating devices to make living easier and the clerk by tending to our needs. Maybe the fact that we also receive for what we give is just a part of the relationship of humanity." He had the urge to expound upon this thought to Lorie but changed the subject when she made some silly remark like "Did you know, Grandpa that all telephones have a receiver but no giver."

"Yes, I know, Matilda," Alph replied.

Alph's Barber

Barbara gave me haircuts for over thirty years.

One of Alph's favorite town people was his barber who, after a mild heart attack, decided to retire within a mile of Alph. Soon the two enjoyed long afternoons fishing and talking about silly things and unusual ideas and inventions. Periodically the two old men would set out to town like a couple of crooks on a devious mission. One scheme the two especially enjoyed was creating large "ESTATE SALE" signs. On a corner in town they placed one of the signs in the ground with a giant arrow pointing to the right. A mile or so to the right they placed another sign with a similar arrow pointing to the right; and another mile and another sign, until they had created a square. The barber delighted in parking near the signs and watching cars go round and round. The first Saturday he observed one frustrated woman drive the circuit four times.

That winter they spent much time together working on experimental material, carvings, and especially creating new schemes for the coming spring. Sadly the barber didn't make it to spring, but died in his sleep on a cold January night. He had entrusted Alph to be the executor of his will. In good faith, Alph followed its instructions with care. The funeral was a beautiful service attended by many long-time customers of the barber. The will instructed that there be no graveside ceremony but, instead, a party at a town ballroom open to the public for a free dinner, libations, and a dance. The party turned out to be just what the barber wished, a rollicking good time.

In the following months several of the barber's out-of-town relatives and friends came to town to pay their last respects. Many of them became quite confused. There were several cemeteries in and around town and Alph's barber had a tombstone in each.

Zed

I could relate to the Alph's eccentric friend, Zed.

One morning Zed backed his car out of its garage onto the asphalt driveway and carefully jacked its rear onto several sturdy wooden blocks. He then started the motor, put the transmission in gear and gazed in satisfaction as the wheels spun effortlessly in the air. He let it run for several hours. This became a daily routine and aroused the curiosity of neighbors, but none mustered the courage to ask Zed its purpose. That is until a visitor naively strolled by one morning and inquired. The conversation went something like this.

Visitor: "What are you doing this for?"

Zed: "Oh, for about three hours a day."

Visitor: "No, no. I mean why are you doing this?"

Zed: "Because I get a lot better gas mileage with the wheels off the ground. Less weight, you see."

Visitor: "But you don't go anywhere!"

Zed: "Yes, I know, and that saves a lot of wear on the tires."

Visitor: "But you don't get anywhere, like into town."

Zed: "That's another good thing. Whenever I go to town I spend money and when I get back my car is right here, exactly where I started. You see, I save money by eliminating the middle man."

Visitor: "You know, that makes no sense at all."

Zed (after a deep ponder and scratch of his head): "You know, you are right. Thanks a lot."

Aaron's Story

It was tempting to avoid reality and hope for miracles.

Aaron was despondent and had to get away. Though he was a sensitive and idealistic young man, he had become discouraged with the sterile routine of city life. Aaron knew that he must muster the courage to make some changes but felt alone and afraid. He needed some sort of impetus or sign of encouragement. He drove out of Chicago, past the suburbs and O'Hare airport, to a small park that bordered a little lake. Sitting on an old wooden bench, he peered longingly into the overcast sky as if waiting for a message from above.

Then, as if a miracle, the clouds parted exposing a single bright star. "Wow!" thought Aaron, "What a blessing!" He instantly became exhilarated and jumped up and down for joy. This single star, his star, filled his mind and body with energy and hope. "Thank you, thank you," he yelled joyously to the sky.

But his spirits were raised for only moments. His star was moving and getting larger and then disappeared behind the tree-tops to land at O'Hare field.

A Dandy Brew

Back to my old friends Alph and Zed.

Old Zed had some big project in the works that winter but it was shrouded in secrecy. The only clue was in his asking Alph and other neighbors to save their empty quart soda bottles for him. When questioned, which was always a risk when dealing with Zed, he alluded to a project involving "pop" art. "Was he making artwork or furniture from empty bottles?" thought Alph.

Alph got his answer in the spring when Zed visited him carrying two bottles of a bright yellow liquid. "Want to buy a bottle of Chateau Zed?" he asked. Indeed a bright blue label on each bottle bore this name along with a secondary line of "A Dandy Brew." Now it became clear what Zed had been working on that winter. It was the distilled result of the dandelions he had so speedily removed from his lawn the previous fall.

"Look," implored Alph, "come in and sit down. I have to talk with you." Zed agreed only if Alph would sample his product as they talked. "Whoa," exclaimed Alph after one sip. "This'll burn the hair off your tongue! But it does have a unique tang."

"That's called 'bouquet,'" insisted Zed. "But what do you want to talk about? I'm in a hurry, got twelve cases to sell."

In a kindly but very stem voice Alph explained that it was not only illegal to brew alcohol but a felony to sell it. "You have to stop!" he exclaimed, "You could go to jail!" Zed scratched his head in thought for a few minutes and then rationalized that he was doing nothing different than those who put alcohol in perfumes or liniments. Alph explained at length that perfumes and liniments were legitimate because they were not for human consumption. Finally and begrudgingly Zed left and agreed to cease his brewing pursuits.

The very next morning Alph got another visit from Zed who again was carrying two bottles of yellow liquid but this time with bright red labels.

"Whew!" exclaimed Alph. "What's that smell?" He sniffed Zed's greasy white hair, which was usually dry and shaggy, and took a big whiff. "Wow!"

Enthusiastically Zed asked, "Wanna buy some hair tonic?"

Once again Zed was forced to sit down and listen to Alph's gentle admonitions. This seemed to conclude the episode, except that on several cold nights during the next winter, Alph and a few older neighbors visited Zed and enjoyed conversation around the fireside while enjoying several glasses of hair tonic.

Catching the Hare

I spent long hours by myself watching animals.
It felt as if Barbara was with me.

Zed had an old dog that some people thought was as loony as Zed himself. This conclusion seemed verified by the dog's habit of chasing a rabbit every morning for almost two years. Like clockwork the wily little furry critter would hop past Zed's dog as if taunting him. Then a chase ensued that ended next to the small plot of woods where the rabbit dashed down a hole in the ground. The dog, now only a foot behind, came to a sudden halt. For the next two hours, tail wagging, he waited for the little critter to reappear. But this did not happen. Finally the dog returned to Zed's porch for a long nap.

One morning after a few inches of fresh snow had fallen during the night, the rabbit came by and the usual chase began and seemed to end as it disappeared into the familiar hole. But this morning was different. After several minutes in wait, the dog heard a rustle in the distance and, for the first times in hundreds of pursuits, noticed the rabbit emerging from another hole, fifty feet from the first. His tail quit wagging as the dog gazed curiously into the woods. Then he ambled home. The next morning went as usual at first, but upon reaching the hole where the rabbit disappeared, the scrawny hunter ran immediately to the hole in the woods. When the rabbit emerged, he grabbed it gently by the neck and just sat for several minutes, with bellows of moist winter air flowing from the nostrils of each beast. Finally he loosened his grip and the rabbit, as if knowing that harm was gone, leisurely hopped deeper into the woods.

For several months thereafter the same rabbit passed Zed's dog at the same time in the morning but the hound did not respond. It's difficult to know if a dog is bored or dejected but this one could not be cajoled into action. The most he ever did was to make a lazy bark or two. And then one day, the rabbit didn't appear and was never seen again. Slowly Zed's dog became a bit more active in the mornings, taking walks, pouncing occasionally at a frog, or running circles around a turtle. The lethargy he had fallen into after the years of rabbit chasing was gone, replaced by an enjoyable but more placid routine.

Zed was aware of what had happened and was understanding and affectionate with his long-time pet. But he was neither surprised nor saddened. Old Zed had often noted in humans that there comes a point in life when they finally realize that they must abandon the competition, when they have "caught the hare."

David

This really did happen.

One of Alph's favorite friends was a short, soft-spoken man of about sixty who had planned to retire in the community with his wife. But before Alph got to know the two of them very well, David's wife was stricken and passed away from cancer. It seemed that David handled his loss quite well in everyday activities, but it was obvious that he was heartbroken and his warm smile that always made Alph feel good about human nature was tucked somewhere inside or, God forbid, gone forever. David soon developed a back problem and became wrought with pain that was alleviated little by the hands of a chiropractor and acupuncturist and responded only slightly to pain tablets.

One summer afternoon David rolled into his driveway, jumped sprightly from his car and spotting Alph walked over for a conversation. He wore a huge smile, something that fit his countenance so naturally. Alph instantly felt one of those warm good feelings inside.

In no time David was relating the events of the previous hour. He had been to town to a little health store in the mall in search of a liniment that had been recommended by a friend in Maine for back pain. "I asked the young girl at the counter if they had a potion called Alcure," David said. "She beamed and directed me to a counter where in a small corner were several tubes emblazoned with the label 'All Cure.' 'This is great stuff,' she said. 'It's especially good for things like the crushed hand injury that my Dad had.'"

"Oh," replied David, "I'm looking to use it for my back."

"But if you crush your hand you can use it for that too," she said laughing.

"My goodness," David said, "I'd sure hate to have both a bad back and a crushed hand."

"But," she retorted spontaneously, "the crushed hand would probably take your mind off your back." David could not help himself and laughed, not that it was that funny but that the young girl was so sincere.

"Well," he said, "this product was recommended by a friend out East and I'm going to tell him that a girl in the health shop recommend that I not only buy 'All Cure' but that I also crush my hand." She went into a silly kind of snorting laugh and this was too much for David who also burst into laughter.

But the amazing part of this little encounter, David related, was that for the first time in two months his back didn't hurt. And the pain did not return for nearly an hour.

Walking back to his house he paused and turned to Alph with a smile. "You're an inventor. Do you think there may be a way to put laughter in a tube?"

David II

I kept telling myself that Barbara wants me to be happy.

Alph felt rather proud to be on David's e-mail list. David's notes were seldom enough so as not to be a nuisance and usually contained a thought that had been pondered on for some time. The latest concerned National Friendship Week, an occasion that Alph was unaware existed until now. David wrote at length on the importance of enjoying each day, especially when a friend could benefit.

> Too many people put off something that brings them joy because it's not on their schedule or put it off until a later date because it is contrary to their routine. Think of the women on the Titanic who deferred dessert the night before the tragedy, trading enjoyment for waist control. Life has a way of accelerating when you get older . . . days becoming shorter and promises longer. One morning we will wake up and find that our lives have been a litany of good intentions and a dearth of meaningful actions. Do something today that will make you or a friend or loved one happy! Forget the worry and hurry and just have a good time, just for today! Don't let your life be an unopened gift . . . it's not a race but rather a privilege to be alive. We will all be gone in a hundred years! Our plot might not be what we hoped for but let's dance before the party's over!

David was not actually that old but he was obviously having the pangs and rationalizations that plague those seniors who are forced to face major lifestyle changes. Alph was very fond of David and was touched by the note. "What the heck!" he said to himself, "I'm going to drive to town and have a great meal!" He did just that, stopping only briefly at David's driveway to place a large potato in the tailpipe of his friend's new car.

Your Move

Long hours alone.

It was raining and he sat quietly in his favorite stuffed chair gazing at the fireplace. On the mantel above was a carved wooden statue in a stately marble base. He gazed at it and memories returned. He remembered well thirty years earlier when he bought the statue in a small shop in Hong Kong as a gift for his wife. It was raining then, too, and he had stepped into the shop to keep dry. An intricately carved wooden statue caught his eye. Instantly enthralled by the craftsmanship, he examined it carefully and was quite delighted at the price of only twenty dollars. He picked it up but noticed that it felt a bit heavy for wood. The bottom of its base bore unusual swirls of brown. He scratched the surface, and realized that it was actually cast, probably in plaster. He wasn't completely discouraged, however, for he was stunned by the masterful job in antiquing that gave it the wooden appearance. It must have been done by a true artisan. He placed it on the counter and, with a slight smirk, asked the shop owner if it was real wood. "Ah, yes! Real wood! Real wood!" stated the little Chinese man. "Hmmm," he mused, "think I'll look around."

At the back of the shop, he found an identical wooden statue; this one was marked sixty dollars. Upon examination he determined that it was indeed real wood. The bottom had no swirls and could not be scratched. The first statue must have been made from a casting of this one. Bringing it to the counter he asked the shopkeeper if it was real wood. "Ah, yes! Real wood! Real wood!" he exclaimed.

"Well, then," he said, placing the second statue on the counter next to the first, "since they are identical and since they are both real wood then I would like to buy this one for twenty dollars." The shopkeeper protested, insisting that the second was of superior quality. After some dickering the buyer agreed to take the cast statue for fifteen dollars and placed the other one on the back shelf. The shopkeeper picked up the remaining statue to wrap it, but stopped in mid motion. He could tell by the weight that this was the real wooden version.

"You try to cheat me!" he exclaimed. "You put back wrong statue! You crook!"

"No, no," he replied. "We are both crooks, but you made the first move. Your move was to tell me that a plaster statue was real wood. So I made my move by switching the two."

They both had a good chuckle. They liked each other in a kind of a "brotherhood amongst thieves" way, and finally did strike a deal. The Chinese man agreed to give him the real wooden statue and included a beautiful heavy marble pedestal for the sixty dollar price of the statue itself. The pedestal was magnificent and with the help of a few taps with a rubber hammer by the shopkeeper the statue was tightly wedged into it making one very lovely piece, which his wife adored. It stood on the mantel for all these years.

He rose and brought the piece to his chair. While admiring it he noticed that with time the statue had become loose in the pedestal. He wiggled the two and they separated. It was then that he noticed two white scratched words in the brown swirls of its base. They read, "Your move."

Nellie's Story

I must learn to think silly again.

Nellie, Aaron's younger sister, also lived in Chicago. She had moved from their small northern Minnesota hometown just two months ago and was still adjusting to the pace of the big city. Nellie was naive in urban ways but was intent on adjusting to show her parents that she could survive by herself. Keeping the job that it had taken her a month to find was very important and she worked very diligently to please her boss. She was actually a bit frightened of him because of his reputation for firing people with little cause. Everything went fine until, one day, disaster struck.

There had been a brief power outage during the night and Nellie's alarm clock lost a half hour. She didn't realize she was late until she noticed the big clock in front of the main offices. She tried to slip in unnoticed but became frozen with fright when she saw her boss waiting at her station.

"Why are you late?" he demanded in an angry voice.

Nellie was so scared she couldn't think. The words just popped out of her mouth. "I'm sorry sir, but my dog ate my car."

The stories end here but my love
and thoughts of Barbara continue.
Some time ago I found it fun and comforting
to resume making at least one Out-Of-Synch
story or cartoon or silly poem every day.
I have a hunch that she's laughing.